The Disappearance

❖ **GILLIAN CHAN** ❖

annick press
toronto + berkeley

Cover art/design by Kong Njo
Edited by Lorissa Sengara
Designed by Kong Njo

Annick Press Ltd.

We acknowledge the support of the Canada Council for the Arts and the
Ontario Arts Council, and the participation of the Government of Canada/
la participation du gouvernement du Canada for our publishing activities.

Canadä

Cataloging in Publication

Chan, Gillian, author
    The disappearance / Gillian Chan.

Issued in print and electronic formats.
ISBN 978-1-55451-983-5 (hardcover).–ISBN 978-1-55451-982-8 (softcover).–
ISBN 978-1-55451-985-9 (EPUB).–ISBN 978-1-55451-984-2 (PDF)

    I. Title.

PS8555.H39243D57 2017   jC813'.54   C2017-901686-5
                                     C2017-901687-3

Cover photos: Forest © iStockphoto.com/anneleven;
Shadowy silhouette of man © iStockphoto.com/xrrr

Published in the U.S.A. by Annick Press (U.S.) Ltd.
Distributed in Canada by University of Toronto Press.
Distributed in the U.S.A. by Publishers Group West.

Printed in Canada

Visit us at: www.annickpress.com
Visit Gillian Chan at: www.gillianchan.com

Also available in e-book format. Please visit www.annickpress.com/
ebooks.html for more details. Or scan

For my two favorite Chan boys

—G.C.

"So you've found nothing, right?"

I was tired of the mind games they'd been playing, thought I'd liven things up a bit by changing tactics. Up until then I'd been giving them the silent treatment, keeping my lips clamped tight shut whenever they asked a question, not even breathing hard in case they thought they were getting to me.

Because I look like such a thug and, I'll admit it, act like one most of the time, I knew these cops would be like everyone else and think that I was dumb as a rock, but there's not a lot I don't understand. You'd be surprised how much people say in front of me, particularly people in charge, because they think it'll go over my head. It suits me just fine, and I work hard not to let on how smart I actually am. If I have to say anything, I keep it short and simple. Grunts are useful, too.

Not saying anything for nearly four hours hadn't been a problem. It was totally pissing off the cops, so now that I had spoken it was pathetic to see the wave of relief that visibly swept over them. It was like they had a neon sign over their heads saying, "The little bastard's finally cracked."

Only I hadn't.

I went straight back into silent mode while they pounded me with questions.

"What should we have found, Mike?"

"Come on, tell us where Jacob is."

"We know you left the group home together. Matt said you ran after you nearly killed Paddy."

I fought down a smile. They'd let slip two things that made me happy. First, Matt had come through for us. He said he'd give us two hours and he had. Second, Paddy was alive. I'm usually good at justifying my actions—I've had to learn to be—but beating the shit out of Paddy was different because of what it said about me. I had hardly dared to think about it. The fear that I had killed him, and concern over what might happen to me, surfaced every so often, filling my mind with waves of panic and making me feel as if I were being hollowed out. Now, I had just a tiny glimmer of hope. All I had to do was hold on and find a way to construct a story about what had happened to Jacob that didn't make me seem totally crazy, one that would make sense to people who hadn't experienced what I had. There was no real evidence of anything, and I hoped that once they realized this, I might just be allowed back to Medlar House. I needed to go back; I still had Adam to think about. He needed me, and I'd made a promise to Jacob that I'd take care of Adam, too.

"Where did you go, Mike? You were gone for two

days. We know you went to Dundas the first night and that Jacob was with you. A woman in the donut store called the tip line after we put your photograph on the news. She said you'd both been there. Said you bought some hot chocolate and donuts—supplies, eh? Planning to camp out, maybe?"

It was the ugly one asking the bulk of the questions. She looked tough: her face was weathered and she was built like a brick shithouse. I'd bet that she was a match for most of the criminals who came her way. She was being the good cop. It was almost funny; she was trying to make like she was motherly and it was so obviously alien to her. She was making her voice sound kind, but I could see the effort this was taking, and she couldn't always keep her frustration from showing. The other one wasn't making any effort to disguise his feelings. He looked at me like I was a piece of wet dog crap he'd found on his shoe. He was smooth-looking, all well-cut suit and carefully styled hair. I could tell that he wanted to beat the crap out of me, not waste time trying to make nice. What he didn't know was that if he tried, he'd only land one blow because I'd have him. Not only am I big and strong for my age, I'm fast, too.

"Did you *do* something to Jacob?" Pretty Boy smiled at me. There was an insinuation in those words: the way he said "do" made it clear what he was hinting at.

I didn't let myself react, just smiled at him. It got right up his nose and I saw his fists clench. When he saw me notice this, he quickly pulled his hands under the tabletop. The social worker who had been called in to be my "appropriate adult" while I was being questioned shifted uneasily in his seat. I looked at him but he kept his eyes on the cop. I gave him marks for that. He was letting Pretty Boy know that he had his number.

Ugly tried again, picking up where she left off. "The next day, early evening, you surface in Hamilton, panhandling outside the train station, but Jacob's not with you anymore."

"You blew it there, didn't you, you little punk?" Pretty Boy smirked at me. "Turned nasty when someone refused you. Not very smart, was it? Because when the police came, they recognized you." He laughed. "Not that you're hard to recognize, not with that face."

The social worker spoke up then. "Enough! There's no need for that. Keep your insults to yourself." He was a runty-looking guy, but he'd set his jaw and was keeping up his death stare. I was beginning to like him. He might look like someone's kindly old uncle, but he had balls.

Pretty Boy matched his glare and continued. "So that's how you ended up back here with us. Now, cut the crap. Tell us what happened to Jacob."

I smiled again, couldn't help it, because he was the one who wasn't being very smart. I mean, wasn't it obvious that I'd wanted to be picked up at that point? "Turned nasty" didn't even begin to describe what I did. It was beautiful—loud and dramatic, a complete meltdown: spit and four-letter words flying, I'd grabbed some old geezer by the lapels, shaken him, and kept hold of him until some passersby rushed to his aid. Then I let myself be overpowered, which for someone my size is a bit of a joke.

Jacob was long gone by then.

They'll never find him, not ever, no matter how hard they look.

That's good.

Knowing that, I can stand whatever crap they throw at me. So maybe it's all right to talk. Only I think I'll keep them waiting a bit longer. Why? Because it amuses the hell out of me to piss them off, and because, more importantly, I have to get it straight in my head first. If I am honest, I'm not really sure what happened to Jacob. All I know is that he is gone and, most important of all, he is safe.

Chapter One

Jacob was already at Medlar House when I got there, last chance ringing in my ears.

Only I didn't really know what they meant by that. Last chance? Where the fuck were they going to send me if I messed up here? It was just a vague threat meant to make me toe their line, behave better. Trouble was, I didn't want to. I'm angry and nothing can change that.

When they took me away from Mom three years ago, I'd gone the foster-parenting route. With foster parents, there's two types. There are the ones who are in it for the money. They couldn't give a shit about their charges, so if you cause trouble you quickly become more trouble than you're worth to them. There's a cold honesty in that I kinda like, but not enough to make their lives easy. Why should I? No one does that for me. The other type is the do-gooders, the ones who are convinced that they can reach and save the disfigured, emotionally damaged kid. That might work with some. It won't work with me. No one can bring my brother back.

After three failed foster home attempts, they gave up and sent me to my first group home. That one was all right. In fact, it was a hell of a lot better than the foster homes. With more kids around I could float under the radar a little. My plan was to just wait it out until I was eighteen and out on my own. But there was a bit of a scandal, a huge media fuss, and the place got closed down. Without going into details, let's just say that "grope home" might have been a better name for it. Someone even tried it on with me, and I had to get physical, which wasn't appreciated.

So this place, Medlar House, was a bit of an un-known quantity. I figured that it would be the usual dump for kids like me whose parents couldn't handle them, or for kids with problems, or for those unlucky schmucks who just had nowhere else to go. Lucy, who had processed me, made nice with my Children's Aid Society worker, took me down to the main lounge area so I could meet the other kids. Well, I'm sure that's what she intended, but I had other plans. If everyone was there, I could have a look-see and try and work out which of them were going to be stupid enough to give me any trouble.

It was late afternoon. When I'd been up in my room, unpacking, I'd heard a clatter and voices. It was obvious that the various schools the inmates attended had let out and everyone was home. The room Lucy took me down to was medium-sized, packed with scuffed-up furniture and maybe six kids. Most of them stopped what they were doing as soon as they saw me trailing in after Lucy, all of them giving me the once-over in their own way. There were a couple of gasps when I turned and gave them the full benefit of the scar. It shocks me still, and I'm used to it, so if you've never seen me before it can be a bit of a stomach turner.

It starts just above and to one side of my right eye, then carries on to just above my mouth. You're probably thinking that it's just a red line, maybe a little bit raised. Nah, it's not like that. I overheard one of the nurses in the hospital say that it looked like someone had sliced the whole right side of my face off, and you know what, that's about it. Back then Danny was a bit taller than me, and when he brought the cleaver down in a swinging arc from over his head, it just sliced through everything, taking flesh and muscle, shattering my eye socket. It doesn't hurt—not anymore. I was lucky that the doctors managed to save my eye. They did as good a job as they could—rebuilding my eye socket and cheekbone with prosthetics, covering them with a skin graft—but it's the absence of flesh that's the shocker. When you hear the word "cheek," you expect a bit of meat even on the thinnest face, but what I have is a sort of declivity: I like that word, picked it up from my plastic surgeon. He promised great things: that he could, in time, and with many operations, get me looking halfway decent again. I told him no. Make me functional and leave it at that. I never looked halfway decent, so why start now? It was hard because I had to kick up an almighty stink, and the only way to convince them to leave me alone was to pretend that I was terrified of more operations. A little bit of fake hysteria goes a long way, especially from someone my size who can do a hell of a lot of damage flailing around. My ugly mutt; that's what my mom called me when I was little, and Mutt became my nickname. It's what Jon always called me, too, right from when he was a little kid who couldn't say "Michael." I liked it, only started to hate it when Danny picked up on it and started to use it because he meant it.

Danny. Now, he's the other reason I didn't want the surgeon messing around trying to make me look better. I want people to remember what Danny did. Yeah, yeah, I know he's serving time up in Kingston, but people forget, don't they? Time heals everything and all that crap. If I keep my face like this, then there's always going to be a reminder, one specially aimed at her—my mother, the one who brought

Danny into our lives in the first place, laughing about how he would be our new dad.

Oh shit, I'm digressing big time, aren't I? I get into a loop sometimes thinking about what happened that December afternoon three years ago when Danny killed my brother, Jon. It's another reason I don't like to talk much. I'm always afraid that I will tell everyone I meet that story.

So, where was I? Yeah, the scar, the other kids at Medlar House seeing it for the first time. Some of them looked away. I knew that they wouldn't give me any trouble. There was one boy, though, who kept staring at me. I could see he was taking his time, his way of showing that he was tough, that I didn't scare him.

"It's Frankenstein's monster," he said with a sneer.

"Paddy!" Lucy sounded outraged. Some of the ones who had looked away got their courage back and sniggered. She glared at them until the laughter stopped.

I was impressed. An insult that got it right—I was the monster, not Frankenstein. This guy was smart. I *was* going to have to sort him out, but later, when Lucy wasn't around. For now, I didn't say anything. All I did was smile, and a smile from me is a horror show. The skin around my mouth, which is mottled red, pulls up in an unnatural way, too many teeth show, and you can see the outline of all the bones.

He looked away.

"This is Mike McCallum." Lucy had gone into full introduction mode. "He's come to us from Mississauga and will be in ninth grade." At least she didn't add the kind of crap they normally do, like, "I know that you will all make him welcome." Like hell. I knew that in a place like this the object was survival, and that anyone new was going to be judged according to what kind of threat they might represent or whether they could be bullied, depending on where you saw yourself in the pecking order.

There were a few mumbled hellos, and then Lucy said, "Well, I'll leave you to get to know everyone. I've got to go help Chaz get dinner together." Judging from the disgusting smells that were starting to drift into the room, Chaz needed all the help he could get.

Once she'd left, there was this leaden silence. I half expected the boy called Paddy to try something, get me in trouble on my first day, but he turned away and got into a conversation with a thin, rat-faced boy with a half-assed afro. I decided that I'd better make it clear how things were going to be, so I sauntered over to the stained sofa that sat in front of the TV. I grabbed the remote from a little kid and clicked through to see what crap programming they had, then waited for the protests that I knew would come when I settled on a twenty-four-hour news channel rather than the garish cartoon they had been watching.

It was then that I saw him. The TV was on a table that had been placed in a corner of the room, creating a small, triangular space behind it. When I'd been standing up, he was invisible, but now that I was sitting and staring directly at the TV, I could see that a boy was crammed into that space. He was sitting on the floor, his back pressed up against the back of the television set. I couldn't see his head or his face, but from the way his back curved, and the way his knees were drawn up, he probably had his head down, resting on his knees.

"Wha..at?" I yelled. "Who the hell is that?'

"That's Jacob," Paddy answered, adding maliciously, "He was the house freak, until you came."

I let the last part go. The boy hiding behind the TV was way too interesting. His posture screamed that he was trying to shut out everything around him, a feeling I knew only too well.

"Why's he there?"

Paddy laughed. "Jacob tries to pretend that nothing here exists." He looked slyly at me and then moved closer to the television. There was a bowl of fruit on a nearby coffee table. Fruit that had definitely seen better days, shriveled up apples and oranges whose skins looked leathery. Paddy picked up one of the apples, hefted it in his hand, then leaned over the television, raised his right hand, and dashed the apple straight down on the kid's head. I knew he'd thrown it hard because I could see how he nearly lost his balance, the force of the throw pulling him forward. The apple had been half rotten and collapsed on impact, leaving brown mush in the kid's hair.

He didn't even flinch.

I was impressed.

Paddy reached for another apple, but I stopped him. "Okay, I get it, but you're blocking the TV so move your scrawny ass!"

For a second, I thought he was going to say no, but he shifted gears fast when I lurched menacingly in his direction.

Dinner wasn't for about forty minutes, so I had plenty of time to watch this Jacob, and I swear he didn't move once. I even found myself peering closely to make sure that he was breathing—he was, little shallow breaths that hardly made his sides move. He was amazing, so interesting to watch that I didn't really pay attention to the news, but I kept it on, enjoying the whining of the other kids about the loss of their cartoons, even swatting one or two who got too vociferous in their protests. I was half hoping that Paddy would try something. It would earn him big brownie points if he took on the ugly newcomer and set himself up as the savior of the others, but he didn't. He watched me almost as closely as I was watching Jacob, and there was a look in his eye that I didn't like one bit.

The smells wafting into the room got stronger, cabbage with a tinge of charcoal, and when a gong sounded, everyone careened off out of the room. Everyone, that is, except me and Jacob and one other kid, one of the younger ones who hung back by the door. I deliberately waited, since I wanted to see what the weird kid would do.

About five minutes passed and then this tall, burly guy came in. He had thick, graying hair tied into a ponytail at the back of his neck. Put him in leathers and a bandanna and he would have been your archetypal biker dude. He looked shocked to see me there, but apart from a nod of acknowledgment didn't speak to me at all. He knelt down to one side of the TV. The kid by the door followed him in as if the tall guy was a magnet.

"Jacob," he said, his voice gentle. "Jacob, come on. It's dinnertime."

There was no answer, not a sign that the kid had even heard him. He looked like a small boulder.

"C'mon, Jake, let's do this the easy way. Jakey?" He edged closer, pushing the table and TV slightly to one side so that he had room to reach through.

With the TV no longer pressed against his back, there was finally some movement from the boy: a twitch, a slight easing of the rigidity of his muscles. He kept his head resting on his knees but turned it so that one eye could see the man.

"Attaboy, Jake. It's me, Chaz. Just me, no one else, I promise. Come on, get yourself up on your hind legs and come through to eat. I've got Lucy saving you a place next to me." He reached out one meaty hand and tentatively put it on the kid's shoulder.

I realized that I was holding my breath, waiting to see what would happen next. If it had been me, I would have lashed out, anything to get rid of that hand. I thought that either it would play out like that or the kid would curl up tighter, shutting down even more. Instead, to my surprise, he leaned into the touch, just a little, and I saw his head lift, too.

This Chaz guy was good. He didn't move, didn't push too hard. Instead, he kept talking, a gentle, rumbling patter of encouragement, and gradually the kid shifted position, unclasping his hands from around his legs, turning to look at Chaz, and finally pushing himself up, awkwardly maneuvering his way out from behind the TV. Chaz rose with him, keeping that reassuring hand in place.

"That's it. We'll just take our time now, Jacob, and go into the dining room. Luce'll have your dinner ready and you can just sit there quietly and eat." Chaz was gently steering the boy toward the door now, presumably to where the god-awful smell was coming from. As they left the room, he turned, winked at me, and added, "You'd better come, too!" I was puzzled that he didn't acknowledge the other kid, the small one who was following him closely like a little shadow.

Dining room! That was like calling a puddle a lake. I'm savvy enough not to expect much in the way of comfort or style from these places, but this was one of the worst I'd seen. The room itself was large but looked cramped and crowded because of the long refectory table that was jammed into it. The chairs around it left little space to walk. Lucy was sitting at the head with four smaller kids surrounding her, all talking away, and one empty space into which the shadow kid zoomed. A silence fell as the whole table looked up at us as we entered the room. Some of them hadn't been in the TV room before dinner and were in the lucky position of getting their first glimpse of me. I flashed them my ghastly grin. It never fails— the gasps, the looking away. I gave a little bow, but pulled out of it sharply when I realized that Chaz was looking at me and grinning appreciatively.

At the end of the table nearest the door were three empty spaces: the middle one was obviously Chaz's, facing Lucy at the other end. The ones on either side of it had been left for me and Jacob. One of them had a plate of food laid out in front of it. From what Chaz had said earlier, I knew that this must be for Jacob, but since I like to make my mark and see what happens when you push, I went to sit there. A small mewling sound came from Jacob, the first noise I had heard from him. I continued to ease myself into the chair, pretending not to have heard anything, when Chaz said, "Not yours, big fella! You get to serve yourself."

Lifting my hands up, palms out, to indicate no offense, I took my time moving over to the other seat. There was a big bowl of what was probably chili (it was red and it had meat and beans in it, so this was a fair guess), a bowl of boiled and slightly blackened cabbage (the origin of the stench), and a platter of rice, all within handy reach. I started ladling out as much as I could get on the plate. I'm not that fussy about what I eat, just as long as there is a lot of it. The noise level had risen again now that we were no longer providing the floor show, and I sneaked a look over at the weird kid to see how he was handling it.

He was chowing down, but not on the food that the rest of us had. I now understood why Chaz had made a big thing about how Lucy would have his food all ready for him. Instead of the red glop we had, on his plate was what looked like sliced ham, some plain boiled potatoes, and, of course, cabbage. It crossed my mind at this point whether I should start being finicky about my food, just to yank their chains, but I decided against it because although this Jacob had been given special food, there wasn't much of it. The interesting thing was that as he was eating, he was looking at me. He wasn't doing the "oh my God I can't help myself I've just got to keep looking at this disfigured guy because I've never seen anything so gross" staring, nor was it the kind of look that is trying to assess someone's strength or weakness; it was a kind of thoughtful, considering look. As soon as he saw me watching, he dropped his gaze back down to his plate. This kept on for a while, like a game. He would start staring at me, but pretend he wasn't when I looked at him. Then it got a little weird. When I looked up from my plate to try and catch him, he wasn't looking at me but rather just over my left shoulder. I was spooked and immediately spun around, but there was no one there.

During the meal Chaz didn't talk much to him. I figured that he had done his job getting Jacob into the dining room, and that now he could relax. I thought he might concentrate on me, the new kid, trying to pump me for information and get a handle on how they should treat me, but, apart from offering me more food, he left me alone, too, which I thought was kind of cool of him until it occurred to me that maybe he was just one of those idle time-serving bastards who have no real interest in the kids they work with.

Paddy, the kid who had thought about giving me some grief earlier on, was two seats away from Jacob, and he kept giving me evils whenever he looked my way. I felt like sighing; even though I knew I was going to have to fight him soon, I just didn't feel like doing it that night. Don't get me wrong. I wasn't scared of him or anything, it's just that it's always the same and I get tired of it, having to prove how tough I am to get people to leave me alone. I was trying to think how it could be avoided when Lucy gave me the perfect out.

She stood up and, in a voice that could have shattered glass, yelled over the general end-of-meal hubbub. "Right, those on clear-up duty, and you know who are," she shouted, looking straight at Paddy, "get cracking and get the table wiped down so we can get started on homework. Anyone who doesn't think they have homework"—she smiled here—"can come and convince either Chaz or myself that you truly don't. If you are successful, you can either go and watch TV or go to your rooms."

Paddy had homework—what a shame! Since it was my first day, I had none. I had already done my TV intimidation for the day, so I was free to go to my room, where I could relax peacefully, maybe read some of the fat fantasy paperback that I had snitched from the backpack of the social worker who had brought me over here. It was by an author I had never heard of before, Patrick Rothfuss. Just to keep in practice, and to keep my legend growing, I shoved and jostled a few little kids out of my way as I left the dining room, not enough so that Lucy and Chaz would notice and say something, but enough to remind everyone that they shouldn't mess with me. Then I wandered back upstairs. My room was close to the bathroom and for once, it seemed like I had lucked out: it didn't look like I had a roommate. Although there were two beds in the room, there was no evidence of anyone else using it: a clock on the bedside table but nothing else—no books, mementos, or photographs. Just about every kid in these places has something that they cling on to, something from their past life, no matter how crappy that was. The saddest ones are the photographs of parents, because in most cases you just know that these were not the good guys, that they are the reason the kids are here in the first place, either because they abused them or because they were drunks or drug addicts who didn't give a rat's ass about their kids.

I have a photograph, just one, but I don't show it to anyone. Instead, I keep it stashed in the lining of my jacket.

It was taken just a few months before Danny killed Jon.

It was on Halloween. We're standing on our front porch, just before we left to go trick-or-treating. Jon loved Halloween, the dressing up, the candy, and he wanted us to have matching costumes. To be completely honest, I'd rather have gone off with my friends and left him to go around the neighborhood with Mom, but he was so hyped about how neat it would be, and there was a part of me that worried that Mom might let him down and that he would end up stuck at home with Danny. Jon loved old myths and legends and he wanted us to have costumes that came from them. I drew the line when he suggested that I should be a cyclops to his Odysseus. There was no way I was going to prance around in nothing but a loincloth made out of Mom's ratty sheepskin rug with a single eye painted on my forehead. So he came up with Robin Hood and Little John and that's what we were: me with an old broom handle to be my quarterstaff and him with a toy bow and arrow. We cleaned up that year when it came to candy. Our pillowcases were so full that Jon could hardly lift his, so I ended up carrying them both. It was down to his charm, nothing to do with me. I just lurked in the background looking big and craggy, let him do all the talking, charming all the old geezers and grannies with his politeness and handsome smile.

I'm doing it again, letting Jon take over my thoughts.

I had just flopped down on the bed with my book when the door opened. I jumped to my feet, ready for any trouble that might come.

I needn't have bothered. Walking in, cool as could be, no one leading him or pushing him this time, was Jacob. He didn't pay any attention to me, just lay down on his back on the other bed and stared up at the ceiling.

Chapter Two

I wanted to read, and so I was damned sure I wasn't going to turn off the light just because the resident weirdo wanted to sleep. It was hard, though, because although he said nothing, I was aware of him there. I kept sneaking looks at him, but he never moved, just lay there, flat on his back, his hands folded over his stomach. He didn't even cross his ankles, for Christ's sake, just brought his heels together. If he had crossed his arms on his chest, he would have looked like one of those statues you see on the tombs of old knights. He never seemed to blink and his eyes were hard and shiny, a deep brown like chestnuts.

I put up with it for a couple of hours, just aching for him to move, say something, or even acknowledge that there was someone else in the room, but he never did. Eventually, it got so that I was only peripherally aware of him: the book was as good as I hoped it would be. There was a lot of noise outside: the usual stuff you get in these places—laughter, voices raised in outrage or pain, adult voices trying to maintain some sort of order. At one point, it sounded like there was a fight, but I resisted the impulse to go out and investigate or join in. Gradually, the noise died down, and I could hear Chaz and Lucy rounding people up and herding them toward their rooms, yelling that lights-out was in ten minutes. I got up and went to the bathroom, and when I came back it was like I had never left the room. Jacob was still immobile on the bed.

"I'm going to switch the light off. Do you want to go to the bathroom?" I asked. I wasn't really expecting an answer. "Okay, your choice. Stumble around in the dark. See if I care. Just don't wake me up or you're dead." I made the threat because that's what I do, but my heart wasn't really in it. He was so pathetic that it would have been like beating a newborn pup.

I have a few problems with sleep. When you sleep, you dream. Sometimes the dreams are okay, the standard weird stuff that makes no sense, like when you're in a crowded place and you suddenly realize that instead of people there are pigs. Best of all are the dreams when it's like you go back in time, to a time when Jon is alive and there was no Danny.

Mom wasn't the world's greatest parent, but she

made sure we had what we needed and she never hurt us. It was just that we weren't a priority for her. Oh, there were good times, like when she took us to Medieval Times because Jon was on his knight kick. Before they joust, the knights pick women in the audience to give roses to, and one of them picked her. She made Jon and me laugh really hard because she was so embarrassed and asked him, "Are you sure?" We laughed even more when she whispered to us as he rode away, "That guy needs glasses!"

So, even if she was in and out of our lives, I had Jon, and Jon had me. We were a unit against the world and anything that might happen. I was his protector, and not only did he make me laugh but he also knew the real me. With Jon, I could talk about the books I read, the things that interested me. He saw beyond the thuggish appearance, didn't laugh when I said that one day I would write books, too. We had it all planned. I was going to be a world-famous, reclusive writer whose identity was a mystery, and he would be my lawyer and front man. It would have been so sweet. Dreams about those times are the good dreams.

The bad ones, ah the bad ones! Sometimes it's an endless replay of the day when everything changed. Jon and I had been goofing off in the family room, trying to stay away from Danny, who was drinking and smoking in the kitchen. Jon grabbed the remote control for the TV from me and ran away. I chased him around the room, and when he saw that I was going to get him, he darted into the kitchen, just as Danny was returning to his chair after getting himself another drink. Jon didn't even see Danny; he was looking back at me. They collided. The full whisky glass went flying, and without missing a beat, Danny made a fist with his other hand and smashed it with all the force he had right smack into Jon's face. When I close my eyes I see that moment over and over again. I hear it, too: a meaty thwack. Jon went instantaneously limp. I don't know if that blow killed him, or whether it was when he flew back, hitting the back of his head on the corner of the kitchen counter.

You know what? It doesn't matter. The dream always starts at that point. I go for him, then everything dissolves into a welter of blood and pain, only to start all over again. There is worse than that. In the really bad ones, Jon doesn't die right away. He just lies on the floor, blood snaking out from under his head like an obscene halo. His eyes are open and he is looking right at me. It's hard to describe the look in his eyes: it's not pleading, more like disappointment, and even anger, and it's directed at me. Sometimes he speaks. "Mutt," he says, his voice weak and fading, "why didn't you stop him?" I have no answer, not even when he carries on, his voice gaining strength as he rails at me, "You're the strong one. You should have stopped him."

His eyes and mouth move, but nothing else does. His body is limp, boneless, and I know that if he recovers it will never work again. He keeps saying the same things over and over, louder each time, until he is screaming at me. Blood is coming from his mouth as if it is carrying the words, and it covers everything in a red film. I want him to stop, but I don't have the words to answer him. His words are inside my head and they are outside, a great wall of sound that pummels me until I can stand it no longer. Then I hit Jon. I make a fist and smash it smack between his eyes. He goes instantly limp. The sound of his voice is gone from my head, leaving it empty, but then it fills up with the sound of Danny laughing. That's when I wake up, sweaty and crying.

Those dreams are the worst.

So I have a hard time with sleep: I want the good dreams, but I have no control over what comes, and the bad ones seem to come more often. Most nights, I want to sleep but dread it at the same time. My first night with Jacob as my roommate was like that. I was probably a bit more on edge than usual because I was in a strange place and had a roommate who seemed to be king of the weirdos: catatonic one minute, out of touch with reality, mute by choice (it would seem), but then functional enough to be doing stuff on his own. I half expected him to leap to his feet once I switched the light off, but he didn't move.

I lay there listening to his breathing, which was even and untroubled, listening to the sounds of the house settling down for the night, Chaz's rumbly voice coming from downstairs. Then I was looking down at Jon's face as he lay limply on the dirty kitchen floor. This time his eyes were closed, and I waited to feel my muscles bunch as I launched myself at Danny, but I never moved. Just stood there, looking down. Danny didn't seem to be there. Jon's eyes opened and he stared at me, only they weren't his eyes. He had blue eyes like Mom, and these eyes were dark, the whites gone, colored a deep red. I wanted to look away, but I couldn't. His mouth opened; the familiar questions started.

"I tried, Jon! Truly, I did, but it was too late." I wanted those eyes to close, the voice to die down, because I didn't want to do what I always did in the dream.

Blood started to trickle from his mouth, his teeth outlined in red, then it was a flood, but the words were still clear, not garbled. "You're the strong one, Mutt, why didn't you stop him?" He was wailing now. His head thrashed from side to side, emphasizing the uselessness of the body attached to it, a dead weight.

My fist was clenching. I tried with all my might to open my fingers, to keep my hand at my side, to stop it being drawn inexorably toward Jon's face. The muscles were quivering. When I felt I was losing control,

I screamed, "I tried, Jon, I tried, but you were dead and he was too strong. If you don't believe me, just look at me. Look what he did to me!" My arm powered forward, but before I felt the wet impact of bone on flesh I woke up. My sides were heaving as if I had been running. Sweat was washing over my face, trickling down past my ears, but maybe that was tears. I don't know. The salt bitterness of blood filled my mouth where I had bitten my tongue. As the drumming of my heart quieted I heard another sound. At first, I thought it was me, that I was still muttering, but it wasn't.

From the other side of the room, a papery, slightly sing-song voice whispered, "I was the strong one once."

I shivered, a shiver that seemed to start deep inside me. I waited, unsure that I had heard anything, that it hadn't been part of my nightmare, but the only sound I heard was Jacob's gentle breathing, so even that I knew he had to be asleep. Had I imagined an echo from my nightmare and, if I hadn't, who the hell had spoken?

I lay there for a long time before sleep finally came, this time a blank sleep with no dreams that I recalled in the morning.

They woke us up by banging the bloody gong again. It shocked me onto my feet. Jacob lay just as he had the previous night. I could have sworn that he had not moved at all, except that now his head was turned so he could look at me, those unblinking brown eyes freaking me out just a little. I thought that Chaz or whichever staff member was on duty would have to come help Jacob get ready for the day, but no, he silently got to his feet and, without a word to me, headed out of the room. By the time I got myself together, he was downstairs, sitting next to Chaz, ignoring the pancakes and syrup that seemed to be everyone else's favorite and solemnly eating plain oatmeal. He didn't even look up when I flung myself down into the chair opposite him.

"So, Mike," Chaz said, "I'll come with you this morning and get you settled in at Dufferin High, do all the paperwork, stuff like that, okay?"

I hate that kind of meaningless talk. Just tell me what you're doing. Don't make it like I've got a choice, because I haven't. If I said that it wasn't okay with me, all I'd get is a shitload of trouble. I utilized the all-purpose grunt, which seemed the safest thing to do.

All of these places have their routines. It doesn't usually require much in the way of smarts to work out what's going on and what you should be doing. Once backpacks had been retrieved, everyone congregated in the hallway. There was a bit of pushing and shoving, but nothing serious. The younger kids drifted over toward Lucy. She wasn't happy for some reason.

"Adam, get over here!" The gentleness of her tone was at odds with the impatient look on her face. "You know you have to come with me now, not Chaz."

So, shadow boy had a name—Adam. He was a sad-looking kid, small and scruffy, a big nose dominating his face. He looked hopefully at Chaz, who smiled at him but gestured that he should go over to where Lucy was waiting with the others. Lucy patted him on the shoulder. "C'mon, Adam, it's not so bad. Chaz has to do the high-school run." She guided him into the middle of her group as if she were afraid he might make a run for it, then herded them out the door.

There were about six of us left then. Paddy was there, the rat-faced boy whose name I learned was Matt, some others who hadn't made much of an impression on me so far, and, surprise, surprise, Jacob. If you had asked me to guess his age, I would have put him as no more than eleven or twelve. He was small and slight and by the looks of his face about thirty years away from puberty. I guess looks are deceiving, though. He clambered into the ancient van that Chaz backed up in front with the rest of us. I couldn't believe that he was in high school: I guessed that he didn't go to school at all and was homeschooled by Chaz, and was only coming along for the ride because there was no one left at home to look after him.

Chaz motioned that I should sit up front with him. Jacob sat in the seat behind me. None of the others sat next to him, but I watched in the mirror as most of them took a poke at him in some way as they went by, "accidentally" hitting him with their bags or bringing an elbow back to connect with his head. He said nothing, but it was like watching a blind come down, each little thing drawing a shade further across Jacob's eyes.

Dufferin High looked like just about every other school I'd been to: a big early-twentieth-century pile of red brick surrounded by a swirling mob of kids. Without so much as a good-bye, everyone piled out. Jacob shot out first like a rabbit down a hole. I presumed that it was to avoid a second helping of jostles and hits as the others went out. Whatever. I was kinda pleased that he had a measure of self-preservation, even if it didn't kick in all the time. Paddy headed off with Matt in tow to join a group that I could tell was nothing but trouble. I expected that Jacob would be waiting for Chaz and me but there was no sign of him.

I stopped, looked around for him.

"Come on, Mike," Chaz said. "Let's get down to the office and get you signed in."

I broke one of my rules then. I asked a question. "Where's Jacob?"

Chaz smiled ruefully. "If he's got any sense, trying to stay out of the other kids' way." He paused for a moment, as if he was considering whether he should say more. "You've probably noticed that he's a little different." He snorted. "Yeah, you'd notice that all right. I saw you watching him last night. I don't think you miss much, even if you don't say a lot."

He was right, but I didn't like it that he'd got me pegged. I just shrugged.

Chaz walked toward the building, and I followed him through the sea of kids. "Yep, Jacob's a bit of a mystery. He was found on the street about three months ago, unconscious, beaten up for sure but no sign that he had done drugs. They checked him out thoroughly at the hospital, kept him there for a couple of days, then sent him to us. The police put out appeals for anyone who knew anything to come forward, but no one ever has. For a while, they thought he might be deaf-mute." Chaz was definitely a talker: he didn't seem to require anything other than an audience to get him going. "But it was more like he had just shut down." He chuckled. "Jacob still does that when things get to be too much for him. Must have been a particularly bad day at school yesterday—he hasn't done the behind-the-TV bit for a while. He came to us straight from the hospital, and it was probably two weeks before we even got his name and age out of him." Chaz pulled open the door that led to the school office and motioned for me to go ahead of him. "Jacob Mueller, aged fourteen, although you wouldn't think it to look at him. He hasn't volunteered anything else. We know he can read and write, but not that well. We know he only likes the plainest of foods, nothing messed around with, but that's about all."

Chaz moved ahead and gave the sour-faced woman behind the counter a huge, shit-eating grin. "Ah, Mrs. Pearson, aren't you glad to see me? I'm bringing you another one of our lost lambs!"

If her face was any indication, another inmate from the Medlar House group home was just what Mrs. Pearson didn't want. She sighed. "You've got all the relevant paperwork, I suppose."

Chaz's grin didn't waver for an instant. "But of course! Michael McCallum, ninth grade, a smart one by the look of his transcripts. Can I leave him to your tender care?"

I decided to play a little and stepped out from behind Chaz, smiling.

She was good. I couldn't tell if I'd shocked her or not. "I'll get him sorted out," she said.

Chaz gave me what was meant to be a reassuring pat on the arm. "I'll be back to pick you up at the end of the day with the others. Have fun!" Then he was gone.

God, the day was long. I used to try to pretend that I was as dumb as I looked, but I nearly died of boredom, so now I do enough to stay in the academic classes but not enough to draw attention to myself. As long as I do what's expected of me, most teachers leave me alone. You always get a few with a messiah complex who want to save the poor misunderstood mutilated kid, but it's easy to discourage them if you're shitty enough. The difficult times are the bits in between: the corridors going to and from class, lunch hour, all those times when students are for the most part unsupervised. I ignore the comments as long as they're shouted long distance. If they're close up, then I have to act. Nothing over the top, just a well-placed punch to the gut or a grab of the throat and shove up against the nearest locker. Most of the problems end there, but if the perpetrator's too stupid to realize that they are outmatched in the nastiness stakes, then I am only too happy to show just how evil I can be. This gets me grief from the teachers, of course, but I'm not too proud to play the poor victim. It always works. The physical evidence is plain to see. Lunchtime, I eat as quickly as I can, then head for the library. Libraries are always safe places. I hunker down in a corner and read until class starts again.

I have to say that in terms of teachers and classes, Dufferin High was a lot better than most. My attention was engaged for at least fifty percent of the time. I kept an eye out for some of the other kids from Medlar House, but Paddy was the only one I saw. He was in the academic stream, too, which didn't exactly shock me. We had a couple of classes together, but he made no effort to acknowledge me. In fact, he went the other way, making it clear that he was ignoring me. I kept looking for Jacob. I was curious to see how he would cope, but I only saw him once, right at the end of the day, when he came scurrying around the back of the gym to stand at the curb waiting for Chaz and the van. He looked a little worse for wear: his jeans were plastered with mud on one side, and he had a rip in his jacket. He was watching for the van so intently that he didn't see Paddy creep up behind him. When Paddy rabbit punched him, he fell to his knees. Paddy was staring hard at Matt.

"Well?" he said. Matt aimed a kick at Jacob's back, but there was no real effort in it and he missed by a few inches, causing Paddy to roll his eyes in disgust.

I'd been leaning against the wall out of their line of vision, but decided to saunter over to see what their next move was going to be.

"How was the ree-tard's class?" That was Paddy. "Were you a good boy and did they let you color?"

Jacob didn't answer him, just knelt there, his arms hanging at his sides, his head bowed. It reminded me of this picture I saw once in history class of a British officer from World War II about to be beheaded by a sword-wielding Japanese soldier.

Paddy and Matt were so into hassling Jacob that they seemed unaware of me standing behind them. When Paddy lifted a foot and prepared to kick Jacob from behind, I grabbed his shoulders and pulled him back so that he struggled to maintain his balance.

"What the fuck!" He spun around. "What did you do that for?"

I smiled and said nothing. I could see the calculation on his face as he tried to decide whether it was worth striking back. Evidently not. He shrugged his shoulders back into his jacket and mumbled something to Matt, who didn't answer, just watched me warily.

Chaz pulled up as I was helping Jacob to his feet and picking up his backpack. Jacob attempted to pull free and bolt for the safety of the van, but I kept a tight grip on his arm, holding him back until everyone else had gotten on. There were empty seats on either side of the aisle right behind Chaz. I roughly pushed Jacob into one and flung myself down into the other. Before I turned to stare out the window, I saw Chaz watching me in the rearview mirror.

"Good day, Mike?" he asked.

I shrugged. Define good.

"Boys?" He was trying the old extend-the-question technique in the hope that someone would answer, as if this would bolster up the facade of normality that he obviously wanted to pretend existed.

"I think Jacob learned to play football today." Paddy sniggered and looked at Matt for confirmation of his wit, but Matt was staring out the window.

Chaz didn't say anything, but I saw his eyes narrow as he looked back at Paddy. The rest of the journey back to Medlar House was silent, which was just fine by me. I sank down into my seat, thinking about how not much got by Chaz. He didn't act on everything he saw, but I realized it didn't mean he was indifferent, maybe just that he was biding his time. He needn't think that I would open up to him anytime soon, though. Being taciturn is what works best for me. It's caring about other people that gets you neck deep in the shit.

Chapter Three

Like I said, all institutions, even if you try to make them sound better by calling them a home, have their own routines. By the end of my first week at Medlar House I had my own routine going, too, which kept me amused and made it bearable.

Chaz and Lucy were the main "house parents." One of them was always on the premises, and there were various other social worker types who filled in for the one who was having time off. They were okay, for the most part, especially since they left me alone. There was one I didn't like much, Bob. He was a lazy so-and-so, and Paddy took full advantage of this to strut his stuff. We were expected to chip in with chores and help in the kitchen. There was a rota and it was strictly enforced. I didn't mind it much. I liked the kitchen work; I had often cooked for Jon and myself.

Lucy, or Luce, as everyone called her, focused on the younger boys. There were four of them—the youngest was eight—and old Adam the Shadow was in that lot. He looked maybe like he was about nine, but he could have been older; he was small. Luce was the hip mommy. Everyone liked her, but we ran rings around her. When Chaz was off and Luce was on her own with Bob to help her corral us, things had a tendency to fall apart—not so badly that there was a great investigation, but let's just say that the weaker ones got bullied a bit more, and if you had something to do that you shouldn't be doing, this was the time to get it done.

Adam the Shadow amused me. I saw a lot of him because wherever Chaz was, there he was, too, and Chaz's responsibility was us, the older ones. Unless we needed to be divided up, like for school or something, Chaz was pretty tolerant of Adam, and never sent him packing. If I'd been him, I would have. It was like having a small dog follow you around, desperate for any kind of attention, just wanting to be liked.

"Mr. Mazzone," he'd say, ever so politely. "What time is lights-out tonight?" Adam was weird that way; everyone else called Chaz by his first name. And the question itself was bogus, too, because lights-out was the same time every night—9:30 for the younger ones, 11:00 for the rest of us.

"The usual time, kiddo," Chaz would reply. "Why, have you got big plans for tonight?"

Adam would give Chaz a smile, then he would start up again. "That's late for me. I'm used to going to bed earlier. My mother insisted that I get ten hours of sleep a night. She said it was good for me."

Sometimes Chaz would take the bait and engage in the conversation further: "Yeah, well, Adam, you can always go up to bed before lights-out. If you want to, that is."

It didn't really matter if Chaz answered or not. Once Adam got going, he could keep up the questions and observations all on his own. An answer was a bonus, but he didn't need much more than an acknowledgment to keep going. I guessed it was just a way of keeping close to Chaz. The poor kid seemed terrified if he wasn't nearby. I didn't know his story, but I figured it was probably going to be a doozy. Chaz was always kind, never impatient, and I kinda warmed to him because of it, not that I would ever let that show.

Adam was wary of me. At first, he would flinch if I even so much as looked at him, but what's the saying—"Familiarity breeds contempt"? Well, that wasn't quite true, but he got over being frightened of me in that he didn't freak out if I was nearby, and he would try to engage me with these tentative little smiles. If Chaz were occupied with someone else then

Adam would talk to me. To be accurate, he would talk at me, because I didn't do much more than grunt in reply. It was dull stuff, the minutiae of his day, but there was a constant—his mother, or "Mummy," as he called her, who seemed to have had strong opinions on just about everything. It got me wondering what had happened to her, because there wasn't a chance in hell that the woman Adam described would have given him up voluntarily; she sounded like an over-bearing, smothering bitch.

Adam didn't hang out at all with the kids his own age, not even his roommate, who was this quiet, un-obtrusive Asian kid. It was almost like he didn't know how. On Chaz's days off, he radiated this lost, shell-shocked look, as if he was thinking, "How the hell did I end up here?" He would hole up in his room if he was allowed to, and when he had to ven-ture out into the rest of the house, I noticed that he stayed close to me. He was polite and considerate, I'll give him that. I found that if I got a book out, even if I was only pretending to read, he would stop his stream-of-consciousness chatter.

One day, I really got into my book and, to be honest, completely forgot about Adam. "Don't, please don't!" Adam sounded panicky. I looked up and saw that Paddy had grabbed something from Adam. I couldn't make out what it was exactly: a piece of paper, maybe a photograph. Paddy was holding it just out of Adam's reach, grinning, and making like he was going to tear it up.

"Please give it back. It's my mummy." Adam was crying now, his tears running down his face.

"Oooh, it's his mummy." Paddy was good. He mimicked Adam's slightly prissy tone dead on. "Mummy would tell the nasty, rough boy off, wouldn't she? She'd protect poor little Adam-wadam." Paddy looked around and was rewarded with some giggles from the others.

I looked around, too, but there was no one else who would help Adam. Jacob was there and watching, but he had his head cocked to one side as if he was listening to someone I couldn't see. Trying to make it all one movement so that I had the element of surprise, I reared up from my seat and grabbed the photograph, wrenching it from Paddy's grip. A corner of it tore off, eliciting whimpers from Adam, but I was able to give most of it back to him. He hurriedly stuffed it into his pocket.

"What did you do that for, freak?" Paddy was furious, his face twisted and red with anger. "I was just having a little fun!"

That made me mad. Isn't that what all bullies say? That they were joking, they didn't mean to hurt anyone? You can guarantee that if I hurt someone I mean to do it and I'll own it. I grabbed Paddy's T-shirt at the neck and twisted it tight, pushing the knot I made hard against his throat. "Well, now *I'm* having fun!"

Paddy struggled, thrashing in my grasp. He was stronger than he looked, and I had to work hard to maintain my grip. He managed to bring a fist around and caught me on the side of my face. Of course, by sheer luck, he hit the worst of my scarring and a bolt of agony shot up the side of my head. I wanted to do nothing more than curl up in a ball, but I couldn't let him see that he had hurt me, so I loosened my grip and thrust him away as hard as I could. I was lucky; he collided with the other kids who were watching this all go down and ended up in a tangled heap on the floor. If he hadn't, I knew he would have launched himself at me and that I would have had to fight him.

My luck held out even longer: Luce came in, having heard the noise. "What's going on here?" she asked.

Adam started to speak. "Miss Evans, Paddy . . ."

I didn't let him finish. "Paddy tripped and fell, didn't you, Paddy?"

I fought down the pain that was ravaging my face, walked over to Paddy, and offered him my hand. He took it reluctantly, Luce still watching us. With my back to her my face was hidden. I bared my teeth at Paddy and then mouthed, "Don't try it."

Paddy remained silent, but as I pulled him up, he mimed slitting his throat. I suppose he felt he had to save face that way, but he didn't scare me then, not one bit.

Luce watched us for a moment, but when I slumped back into my chair and Paddy sauntered off and turned on the TV, she contented herself with saying, "No roughhousing, okay?" just to let us know that she didn't buy our story, but wasn't going to press it any further.

Needless to say, Adam was all over me, thanking me, pulling out the photograph that had started the whole incident. I didn't have any choice but to look at it as he thrust it onto my book. It showed a much younger Adam, no older than, say, four, with a woman who was clutching him like her life depended on it. She looked pretty ordinary to me, maybe a little old-fashioned in her dress, but it was her eyes that were scary. She wasn't looking at whoever was taking the photograph like you normally do, but was staring fixedly at Adam. It reminded me of the way our cat used to stare at birds when it was stalking them in the garden.

"That's my mummy." Adam twittered away like I'd never heard him talk about her before. "She always protected me, made sure nothing bad happened to me, because there are a lot of bad things that could happen." He edged closer, almost draping himself over me. "She said it was us against the world." He smiled, but within a few seconds the smile faltered. "I wish she hadn't gone away."

I shrugged him off and shifted position.

"Was your mummy like that? Did she go away, too? Do you miss her?" He battered me with questions, and it felt like stones were being thrown at me. I didn't want to hear them. I didn't even want to think about them.

Adam was too locked into his mummy monologue to notice that I was trying to move away, to close him down.

"Shut up, okay! I don't give a fuck about your mummy!" I added a push, not a hard one, but one I hoped would get my message across.

Adam looked horrified but he didn't stop. Now, it was a stream of "I am so sorry, Mike. I'll stop. I promise I'll stop. Don't be cross with me. Please don't be cross." He wouldn't shut up, not even when I got up and headed out of the room to go upstairs. He trailed along behind me, and it struck me that these apologies sounded like things he'd said many times before, which left me wondering just how wonderful his mother actually had been. Even after I slammed the door in his face when I reached the room I shared with Jacob, I could still hear him outside. I had wondered before why Adam was in Medlar House and not a foster home, or even adopted. I could kinda see why now: he wasn't exactly normal. The fact that he was just not cute probably had something to do with it, too. He was, to be blunt, an ugly kid. Not ugly like me: my scar took things to a whole different level. He was thin, and somehow his features were too big for his face. He had one of those red, wet-looking mouths that always hung slightly open.

In general, though, I saw more of Chaz than anyone else. As I've mentioned, he was a talker. Wherever he was, whoever he was with, he would start chatting away, innocuous stuff, or so it seemed: the weather, a film he'd seen, the TV program you might be watching. He was good: you'd start by answering simple, trivial questions and before you knew it, he'd got you into the heavy stuff, the stuff you didn't really want to talk about—and believe me, we all had that shit. If you were a sneaky bastard like me, you listened when he got the others going. I learned some useful stuff that way.

Jacob and I were the only ones who were resistant to Chaz's gentle interrogations. I kind of liked Chaz, as much as I like anyone, so I didn't just blank him totally. I'd answer the easy stuff, but if he tried to probe I was really good at changing the subject. I was obvious about it, and it became a kind of game between the two of us. Jacob, though, he was like a stone. He would nod or shake his head if Chaz asked him a question like, "Do you want something to eat?" but anything else got no reaction at all. At times, he would gaze at a spot just to Chaz's right, just staring. I always wondered why Chaz didn't react: Jacob almost looked as if he could see someone or something there and was listening intently. It was creepiest when his expression changed and he would look sad or smile. Always, though, he was silent, *schtum*, mute.

Without ever having heard Jacob speak, I had no way of knowing whether that voice on my first night was his. I wanted to think it was, even though he had appeared to be so soundly asleep, because if it wasn't . . . I shuddered just thinking about it.

So, how did I pass the time and what was my routine?

The basics were school, establishing my dominance, stirring things up, and Jacob watching, although how I carried them out varied.

When Chaz was around, I was a good boy—well, on the surface anyway—contenting myself with little digs here and there. Matt was always an easy target: a whispered word about the sexual habits of his mother (as I said, being a good eavesdropper has its advantages) could cause him to melt down quite spectacularly. To alleviate his anger he would go pick on the little kids, especially Adam, and I would sit back, watch the fallout, and know that no one was paying attention to me at all, which is a good thing when you're naturally the noticeable one.

When it was lovely Luce in charge, I could afford to be a little less subtle; this was the time I threw my weight around a fair bit. Paddy and I were in a pissing contest to see who could call the shots. In every one of these places, there's always one kid who's the boss. Paddy had been cock of the walk until I came along and started to challenge his leadership. After the incident with Adam, he glared even harder at me when we crossed paths, and I could see him just waiting for a chance to get at me in some way.

And then there was Jacob. The kid fascinated me. I found myself studying him, trying to work out what was going on in his head. As I've mentioned, he never spoke. I never tried to make him when we were alone in our room. There was no point. It seemed like he drifted through his days, just going through the motions, but I suspected that there was more purpose to it than was apparent.

I kept a kind of mental portfolio, a list of what I had learned about him either from Chaz or by watching him. It was pretty meager in the beginning. I knew his name, Jacob Mueller, and that he was fourteen, although physically he could have passed for ten. He was scrawny, but not weak. I had seen him stripped down and he had muscles, so it was more that he looked undernourished. He had dirty blond hair, those shiny brown eyes, and yellowish teeth that looked like no dentist had ever been near them. It was hard to assess his intelligence, but I was certain he didn't belong in the special education classes at school. There was this keen, thoughtful quality to his watchfulness at the times when he wasn't overloaded and had shut down. No one had come forward to claim him, but he had been badly beaten when he was found. Although he didn't speak, he made his likes and dislikes pretty clear. His food had to be simple, nothing mixed up or spicy. Water and milk were the only things he would drink. He never watched TV, and if he was in the room and it was on, he always positioned himself so that he couldn't see the screen at all. He didn't seem to like modern fasteners like zips or Velcro, which I thought was taking things a little far, but Luce had even found him pants with a button fly. I had noticed that he didn't seem to like traveling in the van, and at first I had put it down to the bullying he got, but I realized it was deeper than that: more often than not he screwed his eyes shut as soon as the engine started and didn't open them again until it was turned off.

It didn't look as if he did much in the way of leisure activities. I never saw him pick up a book or a newspaper. At school, I presumed that he did whatever he was told to do in the classroom, but I was just guessing. At Medlar House, he would just find some place to sit until we were allowed to go to our rooms, where he would lie on his bed in the same position, always: flat on his back, arms by his sides, legs stretched straight out. When he was downstairs just sitting around, sometimes his eyes were closed, but mostly he was watching what was going on. He never obviously stared, but once I started watching for it, I saw that he did this weird thing of looking behind or just to the side of a person, like they had a companion only he could see. He watched Adam a lot. If anyone looked at him, though, he would instantly look away at something else. Occasionally he had the Jacob equivalent of a hissy fit, "overloads" as Chaz called them. These could be prompted by a particularly bad day at school, for example. From what I could see, Jacob was the chosen whipping boy for just about every bad-ass kid in the school and some who weren't and should have known better. I saw him kicked, hit, spit on, and shoved inside lockers, and that was just in public places. I'm sure worse went on where no one could see. He never did anything in return, but I think he was pretty adept at finding safe bolt-holes. I had the feeling that whenever he could he hid out somewhere around the gym. More than once, I had seen him coming from that direction, and it was most definitely not where the special ed department was. Something out of the ordinary routine could cause an overload, too. Halloween blew his mind: the costumes really freaked him out, and he went limp when Luce took his arm and tried to guide him toward a pile of outfits and props to choose something. I was having no part of it either, so didn't go out with the others, even ignoring Paddy's comment that

I didn't need a costume: I could go as I was, ha ha! We didn't get many trick-or-treaters—Medlar House obviously had a reputation—but there were some brave souls who risked it, and the ringing of the door-bell finished Jacob off. He ended up catatonic behind the TV, just as I had seen him on the day I arrived. When he got in this state, Chaz was the only person who was able to get him out of it. He'd just talk to him, saying nothing very important, just being there, until Jacob felt it was safe to rejoin the world once more.

I probably would not have been anyone's choice for a roommate for Jacob if the place hadn't been full when I arrived. I got the sense that Chaz and Luce kept a very close eye the first week or so I was there to see how I would behave. I think it helped when I rousted Paddy a little when he went after Jacob. I didn't mean to do it. It was instinctive. One day, Paddy tripped Jacob in the hallway and then went in to kick him, trying to make it look like he was losing his own balance. I grabbed Paddy's arm, pulling it back as if I was helping him stay upright.

"Whoa, careful there, bud!" I said. "Don't want you falling, too." I held him tight, and I know that anyone watching—and there were people watching: Chaz, Lucy, and Adam among them, Adam's mouth hang-ing open in shock that I'd dare to take on Paddy—would see the pressure I was exerting on Paddy's arm.

It gave Jacob time to scramble to his feet and move away fast.

After that, and when I showed no sign of doing anything but leaving Jacob be, they relaxed, so much so that when one kid left Medlar when his grandparents came to rescue him, they didn't even move me out of our room, which would have allowed Jacob to return to solitary splendor. Hell, maybe they figured that it was good to have someone in there with him. I was protection if anyone else tried anything and, in the best of all possible worlds (which you and I know doesn't exist), I might even prove to be the breakthrough in getting him to communicate. Of course, I could be fooling myself, and the real reason that we were roommates was that they thought no one else could stomach me.

One thing I had noticed was that I wasn't having nightmares. Not since that first night had I woken up screaming, my sheets sodden with sweat, the feeling of desolate helplessness filling me up. I didn't know what to make of this. Part of me hoped it was a sign that maybe my mind was working through things. Shrink speak. Oh, I've seen plenty of those since Jon died. None of them did any good. I didn't expect them to: nothing they could say or get me to do would change the fact that Danny killed Jon.

Things changed the day my mother came to visit. I was angry. I hate seeing her, but they never let me refuse to do it, because she's my only living relative or some such crap reason. She doesn't really want to come. She's scared of me. That and the fact that she couldn't control me is why I'm not living with her anymore, not that I'd want to anyway. Social workers and shrinks, they have all told me that I blame her for what happened and that I'll get over it when I can think more rationally. They are right and wrong. I do blame her, that's for sure, but I'm not going to get over it, not ever.

She's always been a pushover for a certain type of guy. Even our dad, who died when I was six, fit the mold: a bit of a wild guy who's kind of shady in his dealings with the law; a drinker, because she can toss them back, too; a guy who's quick with his fists, because that shows he cares enough to be jealous; and, although she would never admit to this, one who's quite happy to live off her. I figure she thinks this is the only way she'll keep a guy. In the looks department, I take after my mom: neither of us would ever win a beauty contest. When she met Danny at the local bar, he was working as a bouncer there but he told her he had dreams of being a singer. She fell for it hook, line, and sinker, and it was less than three weeks later that he had moved in and she'd taken a second job so she could help him fulfill his dreams. I think she envisioned him spending his days penning mournful country and western ditties, one of which would make their fortune. Ha! He spent the day watching TV, smoking and drinking, and occasionally surfing the Internet for porn. It was obvious to everyone but her that he was a complete waster. He resented the hell out of Jon and me because we were a drain, as he saw it, on both Mom's time and her finances. If I hadn't been there, he probably would have taken it out on Jon, but he knew that I'd never let him do that.

It's putting Danny first that I will never forgive her for, the way she didn't care what was happening to us as long as she had a man in her bed, one that she could boast about to her lush friends.

Jon was worth a hundred Dannys.

Even when he was nine, you knew that Jon was special. He was a straight A student, but not nerdy. He was sporty and popular, too. He could have been anything he wanted to be, and he would have been amazing at whatever he chose. For most people he won't ever be anything but a grainy photograph in a newspaper—a statistic, just another kid killed by his mother's abusive lover. I worry that if I don't keep hating, don't keep remembering all that Jon could have been, it will be like he never existed.

Mom doesn't think of that Jon. She has two contradictory Jons in her head. One is the martyred angel in heaven. That one is good because he gets her sympathy, but that Jon could have come off a greeting card; he's beautiful, perfect, and unreal. The other Jon is one she secretly hates because he is the reason Danny isn't with her anymore.

I never learn. I should just go with the flow, answer her politely, and get the visit over so that we can forget about each other for another six months.

When she came in that day, I noticed that she's starting to look older. It requires more makeup to cover the wrinkles. She'd put on weight, too. Her clothes no longer fit well, the buttons on her blouse gaping slightly, a roll of fat visible at her waist.

"Mike," she said, her voice sweet, little-girly. "How you doing, baby?"

"Okay."

"They treating you well?" She asks what she thinks she's supposed to, but she's not interested in what I have to say. When Children's Aid first took me from our house way back when, I hated my foster-care placement so much that I would beg her to take me home with her when she visited, even though I hated being with her, too. I'd promise to be good, but she'd just sigh and say, "Don't be like that, honey." I was such a mess then that I wasn't thinking straight.

The pattern's always the same with her visits. She asks trite questions and I grunt. When that's gone on for a while, she starts to sniffle, then the tears come. She weeps for poor angel Jon, and maybe for ugly scarred Mutt (perhaps I kid myself about that), but mostly the tears are for herself, if she was truly honest.

I can't help it, I always bite and say something about Danny. This time, though, she said the thing that means I can never forgive her.

"Aw, Mutt, you both knew what Danny was like when he got a little merry, that his temper could get the better of him. You boys should have known better than to mess around, and Jon was nine, old enough to know that you don't run around playing hide-and-seek."

You'd think she'd want nothing to do with a guy who killed one of her sons and disfigured the other, but she writes to him. Can you believe that? I think she visits him, too. She hasn't said, but I wouldn't be at all surprised.

"He killed your son! How can you make excuses for the bastard?" I had to fight to stay sitting down. I wanted to hit something, break something, just to relieve the anger that was boiling inside me. She sat there crying, repeating how sorry he was for what he'd done, how he couldn't control himself when he was drunk, that Jon should have known not to provoke him.

I lost it then. I stood up and with both hands upended the table we'd been sitting at, shattering the teapot and mugs. My hands formed fists and I had to fight to keep them at my sides. Words were forcing their way out in a roaring bellow as I repeated over and over, "Jon was fucking nine years old. All he did was knock over Danny's glass of whisky."

I couldn't stop. I wanted to fill the room with noise, bludgeon her with words to make her realize what Danny was like. She cowered away from me, huddling in a corner of the room.

I had never felt such anger, and it swallowed me whole. I really don't remember much after that. Luce told me that she and Chaz had to manhandle me to my room, that Chaz forced me to lie down and sat with me until I fell asleep. Luce said it took her almost an hour to calm my mother down. I don't remember anything until it was dark, the whole house was quiet, and I was suddenly awake, chilled with sweat and the memory of Jon's angry eyes staring at me. The dream was back.

Then I heard the voice again—that rusty, whispering voice—but this time, I was positive it was coming from Jacob's bed.

"Danny killed Jon," it said. "Danny killed Jon. Something burst in Jon's head. It didn't hurt but a second."

A convulsive shiver shook my whole body. Jacob was talking. He was talking about things he shouldn't know about. I could buy that I might have shouted Jon's name out in my sleep, but not Danny's. I can hardly bring myself to say his fucking name. Saying it, or rather shouting it, to my mother had physically hurt, like a lump of gristle was being ripped from my throat. Now, I felt like I was paralyzed and all I could do was lie there while that strange little voice said these things over and over again. I should have been scared, and maybe deep down I was, but most of all I wanted the voice never to stop.

Speaking was difficult, but finally, I forced out some words. "How do you know that?" I asked. "How can you say that and sound so sure? How do you know about Jon and Danny?" I didn't think I'd get an answer. Hell, this was Jacob the mute actually talking.

Jacob's voice cut off and the only sound left in the room was my ragged breathing.

I wasn't going to give up. I kept on repeating my questions, whispering as loud as I dared, and adding, "How do you know about my brother, you little bastard?"

Finally, I heard his bed creak, and in the dark I sensed movement as he came and stood by the side of my bed.

"Jon was here," he said, as casually as I might have said, "It rained today." He reached out a hand and patted the mattress next to my shoulder. "He sat there and looked at you. Then he told me. He told me about Danny. He's gone now."

I could feel a whirlwind building inside me, a whirlwind of questions, of emotions. The questions poured out, but now Jacob was silent again. There was a strange look on his face. It was only later, when I calmed down and thought about it, that I realized he looked guilty and almost frightened, as if he had done something he shouldn't have. He skittered away and climbed back onto his bed, but he didn't return to his usual position. Instead, he curled into a tight little ball, hands clasped protectively over his head, eyes squeezed shut. Nothing I said got any reaction, not even when I went over and shook his shoulders as if I was trying to shake answers out of him. When I saw I was getting nowhere I just stood there looking at him. I hadn't realized I was crying, but my cheeks were wet and my nose full of snot.

Jacob remained in that cowering ball, but now he lowered his hands from his head and opened his eyes. He smiled. It was a sweet smile, but it was also a knowing one.

Then I was scared.

Chapter Four

I returned to my bed, but I couldn't sleep with all the thoughts that were churning inside me. What the hell was going on? Was Jacob telepathic, or psychic in some way? Whatever it was, it scared me shitless.

Don't get me wrong; I'm not some wuss who freaks out over horror shows. Hell, my life is one big horror show, with me taking the starring role as monster. I'm not sure that I believe in life after death exactly, everyone going to a happy place or the other place, but I kind of believe that a spirit may hang around, you know, particularly if they . . . shit, I hate even thinking this, let alone saying it, in case I lose it again. . . died violently. It's okay. People seem to think that ghosts usually haunt a particular place, but I don't see why that should be so. The kitchen where Jon died means nothing. Mom doesn't even live in that house now. Why would his spirit want to linger there? *I'm* where he would want to be: I'm the one thing that was stable in his life, the one person who loved him. Or maybe he was hanging around because in the end I wasn't able to protect him. If I was making the right connections, then what did Jon want? Was it revenge, or was it that he couldn't leave?

I just lay there, scared but thinking. I heard Jacob's breathing change and knew that he had fallen deeply asleep. Later, near dawn, I tried to make my mind blank to see if I could somehow sense if Jon was there, in our room, but I got nothing, just a headache. By the time the morning came, I had a plan. I had to get Jacob talking, and maybe, just maybe, I could talk to Jon through him, tell him that I had tried, that Danny had been punished.

I didn't waste any time. As soon as I heard the gong's unholy racket, I was on my feet. I positioned myself in front of the bedroom door, figuring that if I disrupted Jacob's little patterns he might talk to me.

"Jacob?" I said as he got up off the bed and moved toward the door.

He didn't look at me or give any acknowledgment that he had even heard me, but he stopped inches away from me and stared down hard at his feet, watching his toes as he curled and uncurled them.

"Jacob, last night . . ." It was hard. How do you ask someone if they have been talking to your dead brother? I took a deep breath and tried again. "Last night, you said that Jon told you what happened. Can you talk to Jon all the time?"

He was breathing heavily, swinging his arms a little. I wondered if he was going to throw a punch at me, or maybe get up enough momentum to try to push me out of the way.

"Well, can you?"

He looked up then. Those brown eyes stared straight at me. A little smile quirked his mouth. He took a step forward and I found myself moving out of his way.

I stayed where I was and listened to the door click shut and the steady patter of Jacob's bare feet down the corridor.

I flopped back down on my bed, sat there with my head in my hands. I hadn't got what I wanted, but I knew now that I registered in Jacob's world. He had not only looked at me, but he'd also reacted, just a little. This was a start. I wasn't going to give up.

It was Wednesday, and what with school, homework, and people milling around, I didn't get a chance to try again until after dinner. I headed for our room. Jacob usually went up earlier than everyone else. When I came in, he'd typically be lying flat on his back in that weird pose of his, fully clothed.

That was the one bone of contention that Chaz had with Jacob: his reluctance to change his clothes.

Jacob never bothered to put on pajamas or anything at night; he'd just lie down in the clothes he had been wearing all day. It was a major effort to get him to change at all. He washed okay, but after a few days his clothes got that musty smell. It didn't help that they were often splattered with mud, or sometimes with what looked like food that someone had maybe thrown at him. Chaz didn't press Jacob too much, but once the clothes reached the point where they were more dirt than cloth, he staged an intervention (boy, have I learned from those social workers who haunt my life). He'd march into our room with a set of clean clothes, hand them to Jacob, and then stand watching him with his arms crossed. Sometimes Jacob wouldn't move at first, but Chaz was patient and would start chatting to me or do this kind of monologue thing with Jacob that passed for a conversation because it was addressed to Jacob all right—questions about his day, speculation about how he was feeling— but didn't feature any participation from Jacob at all. This usually worked; after about five minutes, it would become obvious that Jacob had had enough. He would mooch off down the corridor to the bath- room and come back wearing the clean stuff. I didn't envy Chaz having to take the used clothes down to the laundry.

Fuck me, wasn't this the time that Jacob didn't come up early! I felt like spitting. Rather than go looking for him, I settled down to read, only I wasn't, not really. I was waiting.

The little bastard drifted in just before lights-out. He looked scared when he saw me.

"Jacob, I want to talk to you," was what I said. Duh! He knew that, and wasn't that just what I was doing! He was obviously avoiding me.

No answer.

His face was blank as he lay down on his bed, carefully stretched his arms out, and stared up at the ceiling, unblinking. I could sense that something was off. His breathing was fast, not slow and regular like usual. He was blinking a lot, too.

I wanted to wring his scrawny neck. He was playing me. I was thinking about what to do about it when Chaz rapped on the door and told us that we had five minutes before lights-out. I stomped off to the bathroom, getting rid of some of my frustration by elbowing Matt away from the sink he was using when I got there.

"Hey," he protested. "Use one of the other sinks. There's no one else at any of them."

I gave him a look.

"Why are you like this? I've never done anything to you!" Matt sounded plaintive, like I had hurt his feelings.

I thought this was a bit rich, since he hung out with Paddy, who was even worse than me. "Maybe it's the company you keep," was all I said, and took a stutter step toward him, fists raised.

It was enough. He moved. Sometimes I wonder why I do the stuff I do. Instead of a nice clean sink, I now had to use one covered with a mixture of Matt spit and toothpaste. Lovely.

When I got back nothing had changed. Jacob was in exactly the same position, staring at the ceiling. I was at a loss. Then it hit me. The only times he had spoken, the room had been in darkness. Flipping the light off, I threw myself down on my bed, pulled up the covers, and waited.

I waited until all I could hear was the faint rumble of Chaz talking to Luce downstairs. There were no kid sounds at all. The inmates were resting easy in their cages that night.

"Jacob?" I hated the way my voice sounded so tentative, like I was begging for his attention. Since my voice broke, I've perfected a deep growl that serves me well, but it was missing in action.

He didn't answer right away, but I heard the rustling of his bed covers as he moved.

I glanced over and in the dim light that came under the door from the hall I could see that although he was still flat on his back, he had turned his head to one side and was staring at me.

God, it was spooky. An image of Jon lying on the kitchen floor flashed into my mind. I had to fight down an urge to run from the room and join Chaz and Luce down in the kitchen. "Jacob, you said that Jon talked to you. Who is Jon?"

I hadn't really been expecting him to answer, so I couldn't help gasping when he did.

The voice was still whispery, but it sounded stronger this time, like he was getting used to talking. "Jon was your brother. Mine was Caspar." The words came quickly and he winced as he said them, even cowered a little, as if he expected me to hit him. When I just lay there looking back at him, I saw him relax just a little.

I was so shocked that I couldn't speak. There were thousands of things I wanted to ask him, but the thoughts and words were whirling so fast that I couldn't string them together in a way that would make sense.

In the end, it didn't matter because old Jacob started up again all on his own. "Jon was like Caspar. He liked stories. Caspar read the best of the two of us."

This was edging beyond bizarre. How did he know that about Jon, and what the hell was up with this brother called Caspar? Chaz had said that no one had come forward to claim Jacob even though they'd been searching like crazy for any family he might have had. Nothing could be found about him; Luce said it was almost as if Jacob had just appeared out of thin air. You know how when something spooks you and you feel like if you were a dog the fur on your back would be standing on end? Well, that's how I was feeling then. Keeping my voice low, because I didn't want either Chaz or Luce coming in to see what was up, I said, "You've been talking to Jon then? Do you see him, too, Jacob?"

"He watched you when you were asleep. That's when I saw him." The matter-of-fact way that Jacob talked about my dead brother was chilling. "I get lonely sometimes so that's when I talk to *them*." He looked around. "I know I shouldn't—that it's bad, evil—but sometimes it is good just to hear a voice, to have it answer you. I don't mean any harm with it." He sighed. "The only thing I like about this place is that Foda ain't here to wallop me if he catches me talking to *them*."

I was seriously freaked out now. Jon, I could just about handle, but this talk of *them*. I sat up and swung my legs over the edge of the bed so I was sitting facing Jacob. It was so I could see him better and, okay, I'll admit it, so I could make a run for it if I needed to.

"Who do you mean by *them*?" I gave the word the same emphasis that Jacob had. I was pretty sure I knew what the answer would be, but I wanted to keep him talking.

"The dead ones," he said, his voice flat like he was talking about the kids in the room next to us. "I've always seen and talked to *them*, but my foda don't like it when I do, not even when they tell me helpful stuff, like when my Grootfod told me where to find his watch that had got lost. Foda tells me that I am not to do this, not ever. That this is the work of the devil, making me think that I can do such a thing. He calls me sick in the head and tells me that he will beat the sickness out of me." His shoulders hunched up protectively.

I hardly dared ask my next question. "Are there any of them here now?"

Jacob laughed, a dry little sound. "No, don't be silly. I'm talking to you now. I don't need to talk to anyone else."

I don't know why, but I believed him, and I felt myself relax a little. It was hard, so much to process. Maybe his foda, whoever or whatever he might be, was right—that this was all made up, a sick game Jacob played to make himself seem important. I *had* to find out. "You said you'd talked to Jon. How do I know that you're telling the truth, that you just haven't overheard Chaz and Luce talking?"

Jacob shifted in his bed. "You believe me?" There was a hopefulness in his tone that was almost painful. He remained silent for almost a minute. "Jon said you'd be suspicious so he told me to tell Mutt that Robin Hood got more candy than Little John." I saw his face scrunch up, and he sounded petulant and aggrieved. "I asked him what that meant, but he wouldn't tell me. Will you tell me?"

I couldn't speak.

I don't know how long I sat there. I think I might have zoned out for a while because by the time I came back into myself, Jacob's whispers were urgent and more than a little pissed off.

"Well, do you believe me? I did talk to him. I swear."

I could see tear tracks on his face. This puzzled me. Why was it so important to him that I believed him, so important that he was actually crying? Despite all the shit that got thrown his way on a daily basis, his face had always been like stone, like he had no emotions at all.

"Yeah, Jacob, I believe you." The funny thing was that I did. Telling it like this is weird, because when I look back none of it makes sense: a boy who never speaks not only suddenly starts talking, but also claims to commune with the dead, and I believed him.

I took a deep breath. I could feel a shiver starting deep inside me. I had to control it; if I didn't, I wouldn't be able to speak, and I had one more thing to ask Jacob.

"Jacob, I need to talk to Jon. Can you let me talk to him through you?" Even as I was asking, I shut my eyes and was conscious of holding my breath. I wanted the answer to be "yes" with every fiber of my body.

"I can't." Jacob's tone was flat. "Jon's not here anymore. He's gone."

"What?" I could feel my voice getting loud. "I've got to tell him that I tried."

Jacob straightened his head so that he was no longer looking at me but was staring at the ceiling again. "Jon told me he was going away because I'd told you everything that he needed to say." His voice was fading as he spoke, as if he had used it all up. "He had to go . . ."

Jacob might have had more to say but I never heard it. I stood up, bellowing over and over again, "You have to let me speak to him! I've got to tell him!"

Jacob flinched and curled up into a ball again as I got up from my bed. He needn't have worried; I wasn't going to hurt him. If he could do what he said he could, then I had to get him to do it again. He was safe, but I'll admit I lost it anyway. I felt like I had been offered an amazing gift and then it had been snatched from me. The familiar urge to lash out and hit things washed over me. The drapes came down in one swipe. I shoved the cheap desk across the room, thudding it against the foot of Jacob's bed. The chair I threw against the wall and watched a huge dent bloom. When I had nothing else to throw, I stood there and howled.

I didn't even stop when the door flew open and Chaz and Luce pounded in. Chaz hit the light switch and the brightness hurt my eyes so I scrunched them shut.

"Mike, Mike." Luce's voice was gentle, soothing. "What's wrong?"

"It's a nightmare, Luce," I heard Chaz say. "I swear, he's having some kind of nightmare. He's asleep on his feet. Let me deal with him. You get rid of the audience."

I didn't have to open my eyes to know that there would be a semicircle of kids around the doorway, all craning for a better view of what was going down.

I felt a breeze as Luce moved away. "Are you sure, Chaz?" She was obviously thinking of my performance the day before, when my mother came to visit.

"Yeah." Chaz's breath was close to me as he spoke. "Just check on Jacob, will you?"

Luce snorted. "It's weird, he's not lying flat on his back like he usually does—he's turned to face the wall—but it looks like he's sleeping through all of this. Man, is that kid something!"

Chaz didn't answer. I could hear him moving around and picking up the things that I had thrown. There was a scraping sound as he dragged the desk back into position. I wanted to stop wailing, but I couldn't.

"Mike, it's all right." Chaz was whispering almost

right in my ear. "You're dreaming. That's all it is, a bad dream."

I wanted to believe him so badly.

I felt his hand on my arm, not gripping or pulling, just resting there. That was what did it. The howls stopped, and I found myself sobbing. My knees gave way and I sank to the floor.

"That's the way, Mike, let it all out." I opened my eyes to see Chaz kneeling beside me, concern creasing his face. He started patting my arm, the way you'd soothe a dog. "Do you want to talk, tell me about the dream?"

I shook my head.

"Okay, then let's get you back to bed, leave it all to the morning."

I let him guide me to my feet and over to my bed. I lay down, trying to block everything out. I heard Chaz move to the doorway, but the door didn't close. He must have stood there for five minutes or more, just watching me, or maybe Jacob.

The truly funny thing was that I could have sworn Jacob really was asleep.

Chapter Five

I didn't sleep the rest of the night. I just lay there, forcing my eyes to stay open. I didn't want to sleep. I was terrified that there would be a nightmare for real. I was terrified that Jacob would speak again and I would miss it, miss an opportunity to speak to Jon. I didn't buy that horseshit that Jon had gone away. Where? My gut told me that Jacob was playing me in some way and I was determined to find out how.

Nothing.

Jacob slept the night through. He had reverted to his usual flat-out position, but his breathing was deep and regular, his face clear of all worry.

At about five in the morning, I couldn't stand it any longer. I got up, not being particularly quiet, and headed down the corridor for a piss. My deliberate clumsiness was wasted; Jacob didn't stir so I saw no point in heading back to our room. Taking more care to be quiet now, I crept downstairs to the kitchen. We weren't supposed to go in there unless we were on kitchen-helping duty, but at that time of the morning, I didn't think anyone was going to give me a hard time about it.

Medlar House is old, and the windows are tall and narrow. It was still dark outside and the street lamps' yellow light barely illuminated the kitchen. I flipped the light on as quickly as I could. I couldn't help thinking about Jacob's *them*. I had this picture in my mind of being surrounded by the spirits of all the people who had ever lived here, and maybe Jon, too. It was only the thought of Jon that stopped me freaking out completely. It was upsetting to think about the spirits of the dead, how they wanted to communicate, how they might be pawing at me, trying to attract my attention. I didn't know what was worse—not to see or hear them, or to be like Jacob.

I shook my head and forced myself to move, getting some chocolate milk from the fridge, putting it into the microwave to warm it up, snagging some cookies, too: mundane things that did a little to stop my heart beating as if I was in some kind of race. Once I was sitting at the table, my hands clasped around the warm mug, I felt like I could go over what had happened in my head.

Jacob spoke to the dead. He had spoken to Jon. Jon had told him that he'd died instantly when Danny hit him, that the blow broke something in his brain. Was this Jon's way of telling me that he didn't blame me, that there was nothing that I could have done? Jacob told me that Jon had gone now because he'd said what he needed to say. It made sense, but why did I have those nightmares then? There were other things, too. Jacob said he had always seen the dead, but he only talked to them when he was lonely. Why was he lonely? He had a brother, Caspar. Where was he? Were there other brothers and sisters? There was someone in his life called Foda—what the hell kind of name was that? Jacob had only mentioned him once, and just briefly, but my spidey sense told me there was a story there, that maybe this Foda wasn't a good person to cross. All of these thoughts were swirling around in my head, and each one set off another, most of which brought me back to who the hell was Jacob Mueller, and why, if he had relatives, had no one come forward to claim him? I was mulling this over, thinking that perhaps he was such a weirdo that they were glad to see the back of him, when I felt a hand on my shoulder. It was large and heavy, so there was no point in doing the outraged spinning around and flinging it off that I would have indulged in with anyone else.

"Mike, are you okay?" Chaz's voice was gentle. His hand squeezed my shoulder.

"Yeah, I guess." I stood up, breaking the physical contact, then picked up my plate and cup and took them to the sink. "I couldn't get back to sleep." I busied myself with rinsing the dishes, waiting to see how Chaz would play this.

"Not at all?" I didn't look up, but I could hear him clattering around, pulling things from the fridge and pantry.

"Nah."

"You haven't been sitting down here all night, have you? You should have woken one of us up!"

"No, just since about five. I got up for a pee and I didn't want to wake Jacob—he's down for the count—so I came down here. Is that all right?" I didn't give a shit whether it was or not, but I've found that if you ask, you'll normally be told that it is, even in retrospect.

"Yeah, sure." Chaz was hovering behind me now, and I could sense a really heavy conversation about my nightmares coming on. I thought that I'd better do something to nip that in the bud.

"Chaz . . ." I hesitated, purely for effect, and when I spoke, I tried to give my voice a ragged quality, which was not hard after all the bellowing I'd done last night. "I'm feeling really rough. Do you think I could stay home today, maybe go back to bed once everyone's gone off to school?" I turned around and wasn't having to try too hard to look tired, because I was. I felt like someone had wrung me out like a dishcloth.

"Whoa, you look like shit!" A tide of pink rushed up Chaz's face as he realized how his words could be taken.

"Don't I always?" I said, smiling so that he knew I wasn't pissed off by what he'd said.

"Sure," he said, grinning back at me. "Do you want to head back up to bed now, or wait until it's quiet?"

I shook my head. "I'll wait."

"Go and watch some TV or something while I start getting breakfast ready." Chaz edged toward the sink with the kettle in his hand.

"I can help, if you like."

The smile that lit up Chaz's face pierced my heart. The stupid bastard thought that some major breakthrough was occurring. Surely he knew me better than that? I did nothing at all unless there was something in it for me. I only wanted to help now because I was hoping to pump him for more information about Jacob.

Chaz put me in charge of grilling the huge amount of bacon that we go through at a typical breakfast. A wise move, since his favored method of cooking seemed to be burning the meat into leathery strips. I'm quite handy about a kitchen: I had to be when we lived with Mom. Ever since I could remember, if Jon and I wanted regular meals, I had to make them. Chaz concentrated on mixing up what looked like a vat of pancake batter.

I figured that since he was thinking I had softened up, I might as well play on this a bit more. "I'm sorry about last night," I said, keeping my head down as if I was too ashamed to meet his eyes. "When I have one of those nightmares, it's like I'm sleepwalking."

"Don't sweat it, Mike. All I wanted was to make sure that you didn't hurt yourself and that Luce didn't think it was some kind of temper tantrum. Your records say that you used to get nightmares a lot. Not so much here, eh?"

Oh, was he ever good. But I was better. "They come and go. I never know when I'll have one. You must have been worried about Jacob, too. Frightened that me freaking out would make him have one of his overloads. Strange that he didn't, don't you think?"

Chaz fell for it. He started in on how difficult it was to predict how Jacob would react in any situation, and it was easy for me to slip in the odd question or comment here or there—nothing that would be thought too intrusive, though. My mentioning how weird it was that Jacob had no identification on him when he was found led Chaz into a riff about how mysterious Jacob's appearance had been.

"You remember I told you he'd been beaten up when they found him?" Chaz didn't wait for my reply. "The police thought he had been mugged: he was missing clothes, and had a black eye and some cuts. All he had on were a pair of pants and a shirt, and he was clutching an old blanket. His shoes were even missing." Chaz was really getting into it, and I didn't even have to make encouraging noises after a while. "Strange, though, his feet were cut up like you'd expect if he'd been walking barefoot for a long time, so they wondered if maybe he'd been snatched somewhere, robbed, beaten, and then dropped off miles from where he came from."

I waited to see if he'd go on. When he didn't, I asked, "So, what was he like when he first came here?"

"Pretty much the same as he is now, only then he wasn't talking at all." Chaz lifted up the bowl of pancake batter and carried it over to the stove, setting it down next to the hot plate. "We tried everything we could to get him to talk to us while the police were putting out their appeals for information." He shook his head. "Nothing, not even when they went nationwide, in case he had been kidnapped rather than mugged. They even sent feelers out to the authorities in Europe."

I raised my eyebrows at that.

Chaz grinned. "You're smart, Mike, think about it. I finally did manage to get his name out of him—Jacob Mueller is pretty European-sounding—and there was that slight accent of his, sounds almost German, so it made sense to try places like Austria, Switzerland, or Germany."

I inwardly kicked myself. Why I hadn't I realized

that Jacob had an accent? I just thought his voice was odd all around, kind of sing-song and whispery. That was something to remember for later.

Chaz had got the hot plate going and was ladling out dollops of batter. "Mike, there's nothing more to be done in here. Would you mind filling up the milk and juice pitchers and taking them through to the dining room?"

"Sure," I said. Mindless activity was good. It gave me more time to think, about Jacob, about what had happened, and what I was going to do about it. The accent thing was tugging at my thoughts. German-sounding. Was Mueller a German name? Was Foda a German name, too? These were things I could work on, for sure.

The sound of the gong shook me out of my thoughts. I could hear the house stirring: muffled groans, the sound of feet on the hallway floors, water being run and toilets flushed. I wondered what Jacob would think when he woke up and saw my empty bed.

I stood in the hallway, watching to see who would make it down first. The front door opened behind me and Luce almost fell in, hastily closing her umbrella, which was dripping on the carpet nonetheless. "Mike," she said, "you gave me a fright. What are you doing up so early?"

"Couldn't sleep," I muttered, not wanting to get into all that again, "so I helped Chaz."

"Well done, you," she said. "I'm running late—the rain seems to have slowed everything up, so I'm sure he was grateful for that."

I grunted neutrally, still watching the stairs. Kids were starting to trickle down now. Adam was first, running and looking over his shoulder as if he were being chased. Then I realized why. Paddy was just a couple of steps behind him. Adam was frantically looking around, obviously searching for Chaz. When he couldn't find him, he threw himself in my direction and scurried behind me. I sighed when he pressed himself against the back of my legs; I could feel him trembling. My last attempt to discourage him obviously hadn't worked. Paddy stopped on the bottom step, causing a logjam of kids behind him. His face was twisted in frustration. Then there was a commotion at the top of the stairs. At first I thought it was Matt trying to catch up with Paddy, but he was nowhere in sight. I couldn't quite see what was happening until suddenly Jacob appeared, pushing and worming his way through the others until he caught sight of me. He stopped, a look of what I guessed was relief on his face. After that he came down the staircase slowly, then stood alongside me, not speaking, just looking down at his feet. Adam made a move then, too, coming out and standing on my other side, still a little too close for my comfort.

Paddy looked at the three of us and sneered. "A

trio of weirdos—the monster, the retard, and the little, sucky one."

Luce yelled at him to can it. She looked as if she were going to say something to me, too, but I just turned around and made my way into the dining room, to what had become my seat, near the bottom of the table next to Chaz. I was conscious of the fact that Jacob was right behind me like a shrunken shadow, but I didn't do anything to acknowledge him. Adam followed me, too, and wouldn't move until I gestured that he should go sit by Luce.

Breakfast was its usual noisy self. A few squabbles broke out over how the bacon was distributed. It was always one of the more popular foods, and now that it was decently cooked for once, there seemed to be even more demand than usual. This kept Chaz occupied, which was good. I didn't need him trying to get me talking about my nightmares again. He left Jacob alone, too, after making sure he got a reasonable portion of bacon to go along with the plain roll he was having instead of pancakes. Jacob had his head down, but every time I looked up, he was peeking up at me, which was seriously freaky.

I ate fast, and as soon as I was done I stood up and asked Chaz if I could go back upstairs to bed. When he agreed, there were howls of protest, and several other kids started clamoring that they felt ill and didn't think they could go to school. I left Chaz to it;

not my problem. I glanced back to see Jacob half risen from his seat, his mouth open as if he was about to speak.

I hadn't thought that I would actually sleep. I was sure that I would have those same thoughts about Jacob, about *them*, and about Jon twisting around in my head, but it was as if someone hit my off switch, because I was asleep almost as soon as I hit the bed.

When I woke up, the sun was shining through the flimsy curtains. The house was quiet. Neither Jacob nor I had any idea of the time until after I got dressed and ventured downstairs. I could hear the TV on in the common room. Chaz was in there, watching an old *Star Trek* episode.

"Mike!" He leaped to his feet. "How are you feeling, bud? You've been out cold for most of the morning. Do you want some lunch?"

I shook my head. I had an idea, but didn't know whether I'd be able to pull it off. "I was wondering whether I could go to the library; I've got some things to look up for school."

Chaz looked at his watch, as if he was weighing up whether there was enough time to actually send me to school for the afternoon. "Ah, go on, I've got some errands to do downtown, so I'll drop you there on my way, pick you up on my way to get the others from school. About three? That suit you?"

I nodded, hardly able to believe that it had been that easy.

"Don't let me down, Mike, okay?" Boy, was he ever trusting, but this time he was safe. I really did want to go to the library.

I ran upstairs and got my backpack and was ready way before Chaz met me in the front hall with the keys to the van.

"Keen, eh?" he said, but left it at that when I didn't bother to reply.

I had never been to the Hamilton Central Library before. It was huge and ugly, a monolithic cube. Once I got past the entrance, I gave a silent cheer. There were banks of computers, and not all of them were being used. But I was brought down to earth with a thud: if you didn't have a library card, you could only use what they called the express computers, and only for fifteen minutes. The librarian at the desk who explained the system was nice enough about it and picked up on my disappointment.

"You can sign up for a card right now. I can do it for you." He cocked his head to one side and looked at me. "All you need is proof of address. You are eighteen, right?"

I shook my head. This was one of those times when my size worked against me.

"Oh, well, it's not a big problem. Your mom or dad can sign for you."

I must have looked even more downcast at that.

"Is that a problem?" I wondered what the guy was picking up on with that—maybe he thought I was a street kid.

Normally, I hated to be on the receiving end of any kind of sympathy or pity, but here I was going to have to play it for all it was worth.

"Yeah." I looked down to avoid his gaze. "I'm a ward of Children's Aid." I wasn't able to fake a sob; that would have been going too far. I snuck a look at him, and his face told me he didn't quite know what to say. I decided to press on. "My caseworker dropped me here. I've got a big project for school and I really need to look up stuff for it . . ." I let my voice trail away and waited to see what the librarian's next move would be.

"That's okay." He was talking fast, happy to have found a solution. "He can sign for you. Where is he?"

I tried to look even sadder. "He's gone to do errands and is picking me back up at three. That's an hour and a half away, and if I can only use a computer for fifteen minutes, I'll have wasted a lot of time. My assignment's due the day after tomorrow." I didn't make the deadline too urgent; I didn't want him to think I'd left everything until the last minute. I was trying to project "good boy" big time. I even managed a sniffle, though I couldn't quite get to the sob.

The librarian rubbed his forehead with his fingers.

"Okay. I shouldn't do it this way, but I'll give you a card now and fill out the application form. Your guy can sign it when he comes in to get you."

I looked directly at him then, smiling and trying to make the smile not as ghastly as it usually was. "Thank you. You don't know how much this assignment means to me. I *have* to get good marks in school." I was letting him fill in the blanks here, betting on the fact that he was astute enough to get my implication that education was my way out of the system. I wanted to keep it subtle, didn't want him to think he was being obviously played.

He smiled back at me. "It's nothing, really. We have to make these rules because sometimes you'll get people who want to hog a computer for hours on end." He looked over at the rows of machines. "It's not too busy today, so you're lucky. When your hour's up, it shouldn't be a problem to sign in again. What's your name so I can make out the card?"

It took less than a minute and then I was off, card in hand, to the computer he indicated. They were arranged in rows, each on its own table, with enough space between them to give you a degree of privacy. There were a couple of boys about my age, wannabe gangsters with low-riding pants and Yankees hats, goofing around on the computer to one side of me. One of them raised a finger to point at my scar, but then I smiled at him. After that, his attention stayed fixed on his own screen. Ugliness can be a powerful thing.

Finally I could start to see if I could find anything that might solve the mystery of Jacob Mueller.

I figured that when he'd first been found, Jacob's name had been entered into all the various search engines and databases, so there seemed to be no point doing that again. Instead, I was going to see what I could find about Foda.

Calling up Google, I typed in the name and waited, absolutely sure that something helpful would come up. Something came up all right: pages and pages of sites dedicated to some sort of fucking stupid acronym— feature-oriented domain analysis. This was not what I wanted. But I didn't give up, just kept doggedly plowing through page after page of results—God knows how many—until I started to hit the porn ones, the ones where your search term was somehow inserted just to drag you in. Then I gave up. I didn't want some nosy librarian looking over my shoulder, thinking the worst, and throwing me out on my ass.

I was stymied.

It came to me then. I had a bit of information that no one else did. I knew that Jacob had a brother. I typed in *Caspar Mueller* and held my breath, until the results page flashed up. They were mostly in German, which of course I didn't speak.

I tried both names then, not really expecting

much. On about the third page of results, I got lucky, or at least I thought I had. There were the two names. I clicked the link and nearly cried when I was taken to what turned out to be one of those "trace your family tree" sites. The Jacob and Caspar Mueller I'd found were long dead, someone's moldy old ancestors. This Jacob had been born in 1850 and his brother, Caspar, two years later. Jacob died in 1890, but his brother, Caspar, hadn't even made it to adulthood. He'd died when he was thirteen, in 1865. There was a sister, too: Katerina Mueller, born in 1862. She'd outlived both her brothers, and hadn't died until 1925. It was her family tree that I was looking at, drawn up by one of her descendants. Funny thing was, she'd lived in Hamilton. That was a coincidence, but it still seemed like a dead end. I thought I might as well print out the family tree anyway, though. The names were unusual, and if I read it right through, maybe, just maybe, it might lead to some present-day relatives of my Jacob.

"Find what you were looking for?"

I jerked with shock. Was it three already?

Chaz was standing behind me, bouncing his car keys from hand to hand. His question startled me, then I remembered that I'd told him I needed the library to look up stuff for school.

"Yeah," I muttered, "history."

"C'mon, Mike," he said. "It took me quite a while to find you, and I'm running a little late."

It crossed my mind that I had my library card and could just leave without getting Chaz to sign for me, but, hey, the librarian guy hadn't been a dick about it, so I felt like I kinda owed him.

"Chaz, I had to get a library card to use the computers and they said you'd have to sign for me, okay? It'll only take a minute."

"Okay, okay. Just pray that the traffic gods smile kindly on us today."

Chaz couldn't resist chatting a bit to the librarian, and I felt a bit bad when he went on about how pleased he was that I actually wanted to study. I shifted impatiently from foot to foot and finally Chaz remembered that he was in a hurry. He dog-trotted out of the library with me at his heels. The van was in a no-parking zone, a traffic warden fast approaching.

Once I was in the van, I pulled out a folder I'd brought, one of my school ones, and stuffed the Mueller family tree inside it. I'd look at it more closely later on in my room, maybe show it to Jacob to see if I could get any reaction from him. Today, Chaz was too intent on getting to the school on time to make conversation, which suited me just fine.

The traffic wasn't too bad, and we were only fractionally late. I could see our little group standing in the usual place as Chaz pulled to a halt, the whole van shaking as he yanked on the hand brake. I was childish enough to give Paddy a big cheesy grin. He mouthed something that I didn't catch, but I didn't have time to think much about it because Chaz shot out of the van like a racehorse out of the starting gate. At first I couldn't see what had got him so worked up. Then I realized that Jacob was not waiting with the others.

I could see panic on Chaz's face—Jacob had never been late before—as he questioned Paddy and Matt. They were shaking their heads, but I saw Paddy smirk before Chaz charged into the school. Whatever had happened, I knew that slimy bastard had had some part in it. I wasn't so sure about Matt, though. He was pale and looked as if he wanted to puke. I got up and loomed in the doorway of the van, ready to stop anyone who tried to get on, especially those two.

"Boys!" Chaz, his face almost purple, was back with the principal in tow as well as the guy who ran the special ed department, who looked scared shitless. "Jacob's gone AWOL. He didn't turn up for the last period, only no one bothered to report that." He glared at Special Ed Guy, who I swear almost grabbed the principal's hand for protection. "We're going to search the building before we do anything else. Mike, get out of the way and let the others on. I want you all to stay put, do you understand?"

"No!" I only realized that I had shouted by the look of shock on everyone's faces. I was too surprised to lower my voice. "I'll help look."

Chaz didn't hesitate. "I don't want to waste time arguing, Mike. Come if you must, but the rest of you are to stay here." The principal looked like he might want to argue, but didn't.

Most of the teachers were searching the school already, some like they meant it, hurrying down the corridors calling Jacob's name, others just going through the motions, their faces telling me that they thought this was a huge waste of time, searching for a kid who'd obviously just done a bunk.

At first I stayed with Chaz, but then I peeled off on my own. Chaz yelled after me, something about staying together, but I kept going, just shouted back that I was going to check behind the school.

I didn't know exactly where I was heading, but I remembered all the times I had seen Jacob coming from the direction of the gym. I didn't bother with the gym itself; I could hear the voice of one of the teachers ringing out from the building. Instead, I walked around the back, onto the field.

Nothing.

The sun was setting and I could feel how cold it was becoming. The grass crunched beneath my feet. I scanned the field, looking for anywhere that Jacob might hide. It was the first time I'd been to this part of the school. I'd thought there might be an equipment hut or something that he hid in, but I saw nothing but two sets of bleachers—sturdy ones, not the lightweight aluminum ones that look like they'd blow over in the first strong wind. These had solid side walls made out of some sort of heavy green canvas. I started to run toward the nearest one, going around the back into the dark cave-like space underneath the seats. The ground here was covered with empty soda cans, chip packets, and cigarette butts, but no Jacob. As I set off for the other bleachers, I thought I heard noises, but I wasn't sure. I ran as fast as I could, ignoring the stitch that was building in my side.

I heard him before I found him, a muffled sobbing interspersed with whispering—whispering that sounded like more than one voice.

At first, I thought Jacob was just sitting in the farthest corner, his head resting on his knees. It was only when I got close, falling on my knees beside him, that I realized what the bastards had done.

They'd stripped him down to his skivvies, used his pants and shirt to tie his wrists and ankles together. He was shivering, his skin pale and mottled with the cold. Snot and tears had frozen in snail tracks down his face, which he now raised to me. Between gulping sobs, he tried to speak. "You came," he gasped. "Jon said you would find me, that his Mutt would save me. The others, too, they said you would come. They know how strong you are."

I went rigid. My brain was filled with the thought that the lying little bastard had insisted that Jon had gone away. It took all my willpower to move again. I wanted to shake him, shake him until he told me the truth, but he was too far gone. I had to get him out of there. His face had that blank look it got. The only difference from when he went into one of his overloads was that he wasn't silent now—he was muttering to himself incessantly: a strange mixture of what sounded like names, English words, and words in a language I didn't know. I frantically tried to unpick the knots binding Jacob's wrists and ankles, but my hands were too cold and the material had been pulled too tight. I tried not to listen to him as he continued to croon softly to himself. I definitely didn't listen to the other voices, the ones that whispered from the shadows all around us. If I had, I would have been too terrified to pick Jacob up and stagger with him across the icy field to the warmth and the light— where all hell broke loose.

Chapter Six

It was shouting. It was faces looming. It was Chaz bellowing and grabbing Jacob from my arms. It was the hallway suddenly being filled with people. It was Matt and Paddy worming their way in, trailed by the other kids from the van. It was the look on their faces: a combination of fear and menace for Paddy as he stared at Jacob; it was fear and what looked a lot like shame on Matt's. It was my legs giving way so that I ended up on the floor, lost in the vortex of legs milling around me.

I think I blacked out, just for a second. I had no memory of moving, but suddenly Jacob and I were in what I guessed was the first-aid room. Chaz was there, too, alternating between yelling on his cellphone to Luce and lambasting the principal, who looked like he was being confronted by a rabid dog. His stuttered apologies and protestations that this sort of thing had never happened before only made Chaz wilder. The word "police" peppered Chaz's ranting and caused the principal to go even paler. Chaz got closer and closer to him, invading his space until the principal was flinching. I thought Chaz was going to hit him.

Jacob was curled into a ball on a cot, a blanket draped over his body, while a teacher worked on loosening the knots in his clothes. He was still muttering to himself. I was sitting on a chair, straining to pick out words, to hear Jon's name, but most of the words were not English. I rested my head on my hands, stared down at the floor, fighting a building wave of nausea. The floor was some kind of tile made to look like pebbles. I focused on the pattern but it was no use; it swirled round like a whirlpool. A flood of acid vomit poured out of my mouth. It didn't stop until I had nothing left to bring up, but my body kept trying.

I heard Chaz yell, "Where is that bloody ambulance? You did call one, didn't you?"

I felt weak, my sides still heaving. The shouting was making me feel sick again.

Fragments of sounds and images penetrated. The ambulance was on its way; they'd called it for Jacob already, but perhaps I'd better go to the emergency room, too. A guy in a suit burst into the room and immediately started talking animatedly to Chaz. I caught the words "head office" and figured he was here to take over, maybe to pressure the school to find out exactly what had happened.

It was then, just as I threw up again, that paramedics rushed in. Hands lifted up my head. A girl worked on Jacob. A gurney held the door open. Faces peered in.

"We'll take them in to check them out." The voice was calm, soothing amid all the bluster. "The little one could have hypothermia. The big guy, who knows. Have their parents been contacted?"

"They are both from Medlar House, the group home. I'm one of the social workers there," Chaz said, not yelling now. He sounded worried. "I'll come with them."

The paramedic who'd been looking me over squatted down next to me. "Can you walk, big guy?"

I didn't want to risk opening my mouth, so I just nodded. He held out a hand to help me up, which I ignored until I stood up and the room started to spin around. He steadied me, then called for Chaz and the principal to help me stay on my feet while he helped his partner load Jacob on the gurney.

The crowd parted silently as our sad little procession made its way out to the ambulance. My head was throbbing and my stomach roiled, so it was a relief to lie flat on the cot in the ambulance. They'd tried to uncurl Jacob when they moved him but without any luck. He lay with his face to the wall, his back curved into a bow. His muttering had stopped and the silence was good. I didn't want to hear his voice or any others.

There was a flurry of chatter just before we left.

"What about the others? What should I do about the other kids?" The principal's voice was high-pitched and panicky.

In contrast, Chaz's was a low growl. The anger was still there, but controlled now. He gestured to the suited stranger with a broad sweep of his hand. "My boss is here. He'll take charge and get them home. You did a shit job looking after Jacob when he was supposedly in your care, so I wouldn't trust my kids to you."

The principal looked as if he was going to say something in return, but Chaz was already getting into the back of the ambulance. Chaz's boss glared at the principal, too.

I don't like hospitals. I don't like doctors. You're smart enough to know why. If I'd felt sick before, the high-pitched, screeching siren of the ambulance made it worse. I could feel beads of sweat on my face. It helped if I shut my eyes.

There's little point in describing in detail what happened when we reached McMaster Hospital—all standard stuff, except for no waiting around. We were rushed straight into the ER, put into adjoining rooms. Chaz did his best, bopping between them until I growled at him to stay with Jacob.

The doctor who examined me was good. He looked me in the eyes, didn't let his gaze slide away from my ruin of a face and then sneak looks back, like you would with the car crash you pass at the side of a road. Nothing major wrong with me, maybe a bit of shock. He was all for sending me out to the waiting room until Chaz and Jacob were done, but I told him no. I was waiting with Chaz. He didn't argue. Wise man.

A doctor and a nurse were working on Jacob. The nurse was cleaning him up, gently removing mud from his hair, cleaning up the abrasions on his legs and arms. The bastards must have dragged him along the ground after they'd stripped and hog-tied him. Somehow, she'd straightened him out from his curled-up ball. He lay on the bed in the position I knew so well, flat on his back, arms by his sides. The only difference from his nighttime posture was the shivering that shook his body nonstop. His eyes were open and staring straight up at the ceiling, but I would have wagered big bucks that he wasn't there. It was weird. He'd shut down. Chaz knew it, too, because when the doctor tried to get Jacob to do some dumbass test, counting backward in twos, he told him not to waste his breath, that Jacob rarely spoke. I think that clinched it for the doctor: he was going to keep Jacob in the hospital for observation. If I'd been him, I would have, too. If your patient didn't talk, didn't answer questions, how could you assess them unless you just watched over them? Before he left to arrange a bed for Jacob in the kids' ward, he told Chaz that he thought Jacob would be okay. He was bruised, but nothing was broken. Someone had used him as a punching bag either before or after they'd tied him up. He had probably been out there a couple of hours; he was suffering from mild hypothermia. The hospital staff would observe him overnight to ascertain if he had a head injury.

"Ah, shit, Mike, who could do such a thing?" Chaz looked close to tears. "Jacob's a little strange, but for Christ's sake, he's harmless. It would be like kicking a puppy."

I didn't say anything. There was no point. I knew that Paddy was behind this, but I had no proof, and I doubted that Jacob would say anything. I'd get him, though. Get him later, when he thought he was safe and had gotten away with it.

I realized that Chaz was looking at me hopefully. "Could be anyone," I muttered. "Jacob's an equal-opportunity target."

Chaz took one of Jacob's hands and began gently rubbing it. "I knew school wasn't easy for him, that he probably got picked on, but he never complained, and nothing this bad has ever happened before. By law, I have to send him . . ." His voice trailed off.

"He hides." I surprised myself by speaking. "He has a bolt-hole somewhere out on the field where he goes when he's not in class. If I noticed that, other kids would have, too. It would be easy to corner him there, with no one around to see or stop them. That's where I looked for him. He was under the bleachers." I didn't mention what else I had experienced under there. No one would believe me.

Chaz was shaking his head at that thought when the doctor came back, followed by an orderly. "Mr. Mazzone, they're ready for him on the third floor, if you want to go up and get him settled. You can, of course, stay with him. There's a couch in his room." He hesitated, looking in my direction but not looking at me directly. "But . . ." He didn't need to say any more.

"One of my coworkers, Lucy Evans, will be here shortly." I don't think I'd ever heard Chaz sound so formal. "She'll stay with Jacob. Mike and I will head back to Medlar House once she gets here." He motioned to me to follow him. The doctor looked like he wanted to nix this, but I glared balefully at him. He didn't say anything, which was good.

When I got to the kids' ward, I almost wished that the doctor had been more assertive. I stayed in the play area near the elevators while Chaz did the necessary. Little kids stare, and they say exactly what pops into their heads; they have no filters.

"What's wrong with that boy's face? Why is it all twisted? It looks like it's owie." This was from a kid who looked about four, and was so frail that you could almost see through him, so thin that you felt that if it wasn't for the metal IV pole attached to his arm he might float up into the air and drift away. His mother shushed him, trying not to look at me.

The kid was still staring.

"I had an accident." I spared him the smile.

He looked like he wanted to ask more, but his mother, in a voice that was too cheery and too loud, suggested that they go and see if the foosball table was free now. He followed her down the corridor, his head craned around on the fragile stalk of his neck to watch me.

"Mike, where are they?" Luce flew out of the elevator, her face flushed with the cold. "Are you all right?" She leaned in to hug me. I couldn't help it; I stepped back and her arms closed on empty air. I don't do hugs.

"In there." I pointed to the swing doors that led to the ward. I thought that she'd go inside straight away, but she stayed for a moment, looking at me.

"What?" It sounded ruder, more aggressive than I meant it to.

"You didn't answer me." She smiled and I remembered then why the kids all liked her. When she was talking to you, you felt that you were the only person who mattered to her.

"Yeah, I did."

She still didn't move, and her smile grew broader. "Yeah, you did, but only one of my questions. How are *you*? Chaz said that you got sick, too."

"I just puked, is all. I'm okay now. They said it was probably shock."

She patted my arm, tentatively, like I might shy away. "If you say so, Mike. Make sure that Chaz keeps an eye on you, okay?" With that, she went.

A minute later, Chaz was there, looking more serious than I was used to seeing him. "Let's go. Luce left the van in the parking lot. If they let Jacob out tomorrow, I'll come back for them then."

The drive back to Medlar House was silent. I think Chaz knew that he would get nothing out of me. I hunched down in my seat. I couldn't face thinking about what I'd seen and heard under the bleachers, not yet, not until Jacob was back. It was Paddy and maybe Matt who occupied my thoughts now. I just didn't get why they'd go after Jacob like that. What was the point? I'm no saint, but if I hurt someone it's for a reason: to let them know that they shouldn't mess me around; to make a point, you might say; or to put someone in their place. It's calculated, and there is never malice involved. Jacob didn't do anything to anyone. The more I thought about it, the more I wondered what Matt's role had been. He hadn't been smirking like Paddy. I could believe that it gave Paddy some sort of sick pleasure to hurt a kid who was so defenseless. He was a shit. That's all it was. A shit who needed to be dealt with. But Matt . . .

Not surprisingly, those two were not anywhere to be seen when we finally got back to Medlar House.

Chaz had surprised me by suddenly pulling into a small strip mall about ten minutes away from the home, parking in front of a dingy-looking Chinese restaurant.

"Dinner will be done when we get back, and I don't feel like foraging for leftovers. They've managed without us this long, so another hour won't make much difference." Chaz turned and looked at me. His face looked drawn and tired in the harsh glare of a street lamp that shone in through the van's window. "Come in if you want; if not, tell me what you want and I'll get it to go."

I went in with him. Mom never had the money for us to eat in restaurants, so I always got a kick out of eating out, even at a run-down joint like this one. Chaz was a man after my own heart, and went for quantity rather than quality. He ordered enough food for a family of four, and we ate it all. I wasn't expecting him to question me further about Jacob, and he didn't disappoint me.

At Medlar House my least favorite social worker, Bob, was sitting in the television room. He jumped up as we came in. "Oh, you're back."

I had a feeling that he really wanted to add "at last" to the end of that, but thought better of it.

I slouched over to a chair and sat down heavily. I wasn't ready to go upstairs to my room just yet.

Bob gave me a look of barely concealed dislike. I

grinned back at him, a big, shit-eating grin, until he broke off eye contact and turned to Chaz.

"Yeah." Chaz sounded as tired as I felt. "We stopped to get something to eat. I knew dinner would be over. I hope you didn't have any problems?"

Bob said, "Well, things weren't exactly normal, and everyone was a bit tense, but I kept it all together." He smiled then and looked expectantly at Chaz like a dog waiting for a pat on the head.

Chaz was moving around the room restlessly. "So, no problems at all?" There was a slight hint of disbelief in his voice.

"Depends what you mean by a problem." Bob's laugh was too hearty for my liking. "That little kid, Adam. He came to me crying, got all hysterical about how he was frightened to be in his room. God, he's a lot to take at the best of times, but when he's crying . . ."

Chaz cut him off, his voice sharp. "Did you go check out his room?"

"Of course I did." Bob bristled. "There was nothing there. His roommate was asleep. In fact, my going in woke him up. Then I had two of them to deal with."

Shit, I had completely forgotten about Adam. I didn't like the sound of that at all.

"So, what did you do?" Chaz was more alert now, his tiredness fading.

"Oh, I just told him to knock it off and get back into bed. If you ask me, it's mostly attention-seeking on his part. He's used to being the center of attention; you remember about his demented mother."

"Geez, I guess you are just Mr. Compassion." Chaz kept his tone light, but his disgust was obvious.

"Hey!" Bob was working himself up to be angry. "I do my best even if I'm not a saintly daddy-figure like you."

"Ah, sorry, sorry." Chaz waved a hand. "It's been a long and strange day. I'm tired, and I'm sure it was probably nothing that got Adam worked up. I'll take it from here."

You could see that the other guy expected more, but he was shit out of luck. He hovered around for a few seconds then started to drift toward the door.

Turning to me, Chaz said, "You'd better get some rest, Mike. I'm going to write up some notes on what happened, then I'll hit the sack, too."

He stared hard at me then. "Are you sure you don't have any idea who did this to Jacob?"

I shook my head. It was tempting to come clean because it meant that we would keep talking, and it had just hit me like a tidal wave that the last thing I wanted was to be alone, especially in the room that I shared with Jacob.

Chapter Seven

It was dumb. I took my time in the bathroom, making sure that I kept the taps running, that I splashed noisily as I washed—anything to fill the room with sound. I kept looking around—I had this sense that someone was watching me—but there was no one. But I couldn't do that forever, and I started to sweat again as I forced myself to walk down the silent corridor and into our room.

Nothing.

It was just an empty room, barer than most. The only reason you would know that it was even occupied was that I'd left a bunched-up T-shirt on the dresser top. I hesitated in the doorway, sniffing like a dog.

I took my time getting ready for bed, again making a point to be noisy. The silence bothered me: I kept thinking that at any moment I might hear voices start up, the voices I had heard when I found Jacob under the bleachers. I had never heard anything like that before. The voices were quiet but they filled the space eerily. Some sounded like sobs, others were hisses— all of them freaked me the fuck out. It was stupid, I know: it was Jacob who could speak to the dead, not me. With him not here, I had nothing to fear. But I couldn't help it. I got this picture in my head of the room being filled with unseen presences. I tried reading, but that was a no-go. I couldn't concentrate worth a damn. I gave up eventually and switched off my bedside light. I didn't fall asleep, though, just lay there.

Then I really did hear something and was instantly hyperalert, sitting bolt upright trying to pinpoint what it was and where it was coming from. When I switched on the light, the room was empty.

The noise was a rustling, scratching sound and seemed to be coming from the closet. My heart was racing and I could feel clammy sweat forming on my forehead. I tried telling myself that it was just mice, or maybe a squirrel in the attic above. Medlar House was old; it could have been. The noise kept on: if anything it was getting louder, like something was trapped in there and struggling to get out.

I couldn't take it anymore, so I launched myself off the bed and flung open the closet door. Jacob and I didn't have much in the way of clothing, but I could see that most of it was off the hangers and covering a struggling, writhing lump on the closet floor. My windbreaker was on top. My hand trembled when I reached down to pull it off.

Adam blinked up at me, looking for all the world like a small rat in a nest of clothes.

I grabbed his arm and hauled him up.

"What the fuck are you doing here? You scared me shitless."

He was shaking and that made me feel bad. I tried to keep the anger and shock at bay and pushed him down so he was sitting on Jacob's bed, facing me.

"Why are you here?"

Adam twisted his fingers together and kept his eyes fixed on the floor. "I was scared," he stuttered in little more than a whisper. "Mr. Mazzone wasn't here, and you were gone, too . . ." He snuck a look up at me. "The other man wouldn't listen to me when I told him. He said I was making it up just to get attention. I wasn't. I swear."

I can't say I felt much more sympathetic than Bob had been. He was right. Adam was a hot mess with swollen eyes and blotchy skin. "Look, it's been a tough day for me," I said. "An even tougher one for Jacob, for God's sake. What the hell have you got to make a fuss and cry about?"

Shit, at this Adam started to snivel even more. "I know. Miss Evans told us before she left what had happened. Then the others, the big boys, they were talking about how Jacob had got beaten up so badly that he was in the hospital." He looked directly at me. "I heard Paddy laughing about it, saying something about how it had been a piece of cake to find the retard."

The swell of anger I was feeling switched its focus from Adam to Paddy. I had guessed that Paddy was behind the attack on Jacob. I fought down the urge to drag that scumbag out of bed and beat seven kinds of shit out of him. I had to be patient. It would be better to bide my time.

Adam watched me closely, his body tense. "His friend, Matt, told him to stop. That it wasn't funny. That they shouldn't have done it, that he wished he hadn't let himself be talked into it, even just being a lookout."

Now that I found interesting. I had sensed that Matt was trying to distance himself from Paddy, and Adam's words seemed to confirm that. I was pretty certain that I could work on Matt and get the full story of what had happened. I didn't really need the why. From everything I'd seen of Paddy, he got off on hurting people.

I must have smiled then because the tension left Adam's body. He sagged a little.

"Why did you come in here? What did you do, wait until your roommate was asleep and sneak in here?"

Adam's face crumpled. "Paddy saw that I heard him. He hit me."

When I looked more closely at the poor little bugger I could see that one eye was slightly swollen, and that he would probably have quite a shiner tomorrow, one he would no doubt explain away as being due to his own clumsiness.

"Is that why you went to Bob? Why didn't you tell him? Did Paddy come into your room?"

"No." Adam was shaking a little at the memory. "I went to the bathroom and he was there, too. He told me that he'd get me if I told. And he will, I know he will." Adam's fear was genuine. "You look out for Jacob, so maybe you can look out for me, too?" By the way he asked, I could tell that his question was born of hope, but a hope that he thought was small.

Shit, I thought to myself, the way I acted with Jacob must have given Adam the impression that I was someone who would protect him. I sighed.

Adam piped up. "I came to tell you. I didn't have to . . ."

He was right, of course. If I did anything to Paddy, that bastard would go straight after Adam, knowing that he had told me what he'd overheard. I sighed again, feeling that I was no longer in control. It was a feeling I didn't like one bit.

Adam's eyes were glistening with tears.

"Yeah, all right." The words didn't come out easily. "I'll make sure that Paddy stays away from you— when I can, that is."

Adam's smile was huge. He threw himself at me, wrapping me in a hug. It was all I could do not to shove him away, hard. "Go easy," I grunted as I wriggled out of his grip.

"So, I can stay here tonight? Sleep in Jacob's bed?"

Now that was too much. "No! You go back to your own room now." It came out a bit harsher than I intended, but it didn't seem to dampen his joy. "I'll watch until you go inside, and then tomorrow, we'll see how it goes, okay?"

Adam nodded and I watched him creep theatrically down the corridor until he reached the door of his room. He stopped there, turned around, waved, and grinned at me. It was the grin that did it—pure happiness, just the way Jon used to smile when something pleased him.

I shook my head. I was getting soft. Being soft was dangerous.

I didn't think that sleep was going to come easily. Too much had happened, and now there was the whole problem of Adam to factor into the mess. As soon as I lay down, however, I fell asleep—a deep and dreamless sleep that only dissolved when I heard the banging of the gong for breakfast. It was weird to wake up to an empty room. Jacob was usually silent, sure, but I hadn't realized how aware I typically was of his presence. There was a timid scratch on the door and when I opened it, there was Adam. His eye was now definitely boasting a shiner, blue, black, and purple bruises flourishing around it. He didn't say anything, just gave me a small grin and followed me to the bathroom, then walked down the stairs at my side. In the dining room, Chaz was already seated in his normal place at the bottom of the table, an empty place on either side of him as usual. Paddy was in his usual seat in the middle of the table—as far from Chaz as possible so he could carry out his petty villainy without too much scrutiny. To send him a message, I walked Adam up to his place near the top of the table, and as I passed Paddy, I faked a stumble and managed to elbow him hard just behind the ear. I was hoping that he would screech and make a fuss, but he was too clever for that. He didn't give any indication that anything had happened, though I could tell from my own aching elbow that it must have hurt like a bitch. Adam flinched at this but made sure that his face remained expressionless as he sat down next to where usually Lucy was. Today, Bob was sitting there, and the bastard didn't even comment on the fact that Adam now had a black eye.

Chaz looked weary: his face gray, his eyes baggy and red-rimmed. I didn't have to ask about how Jacob was; Chaz was talking even before I had slumped into my chair.

"Luce called about an hour ago. They're keeping Jacob one more night. I'll go visit them, maybe spell off Luce awhile. No!" He raised a hand, palm facing me, as I opened my mouth to speak. "You can't come. Go to school." He kept the hand raised. "If it makes you feel any better, you can play detective. Try and find out anything you can about what happened yesterday . . ." His sigh was resigned. "The principal will make all the right noises, but he'll be playing a waiting game, waiting for the fuss to die down. He could not care less who beat up the weird kid from the group home."

After that there was nothing more from Chaz except brief commands. His mood infected us all and, without Jacob there to be the punching bag, we got into the minivan silently and without the usual shoving and pushing. Well, almost. Paddy, coming on last, managed to swing his backpack onto his shoulder just as he passed me, the edge of a folder inside clipping me just above my eye. He smirked.

Playing detective was a joke. At the best of times I tried to have as little contact with others as I could, so it was hardly as though anyone was likely to open up and start talking to me. Oh yes, I got a subtle feeling that everyone was on their guard, but I heard nothing except some losers saying that whoever had beaten up Jacob was righteous because, after all, he was a weird little shit who gave them the creeps. You'd have thought that both Paddy and Matt would have been the dictionary definition of low profile, but no. Today,

Paddy was getting in my face as much as he could. As I've said, he was in most of the honors classes with me, and he took to giving me a little nod and slight smile whenever he caught me looking at him. My irritation simmered. Matt, though, I hardly saw at all that day. Normally he waited outside the English classroom for Paddy at lunchtime, but today he was definitely missing in action.

The day was one huge drag. I could barely concentrate in class, staying just attentive enough that no one would call me on it, but my brain was bubbling like a stew.

I needed to be there for Jacob and now, fuck me, for Adam. That meant that I couldn't risk openly retaliating against Paddy and Matt. I had to be a good boy. If I did anything wrong, got physical with them, I could see myself being carted off to some young offenders' shithole. The annoying thing was that Paddy was smart enough to know that, and I'm sure that made it all the sweeter for that bastard. Even though it made me sick to my stomach to let it go for now, I had no choice. The only thing I could think of doing was to try and find out more about Jacob, perhaps track down some relatives so that they could at least get him out of Medlar House and to a place where he wouldn't be everyone's whipping boy.

Maybe he'd talk to me when he finally got back. I could certainly hope. The only lead I had was that genealogy site, and I needed to get back to the library to investigate it further. Mueller was an unusual name, and Katerina Mueller had lived in Hamilton, and obviously had relatives who had bothered to draw up a family tree. Maybe, just maybe, there were still some Muellers in the area and . . . I stopped myself. It was a lot of maybes, and I could easily add another one. If Jacob did have family here, maybe they were the ones who had beaten him in the first place; maybe they wanted nothing to do with him.

Thinking like that made me careless. I was in history and that was the one class I didn't share with Paddy, so I could drop my guard a little. I like history, and the guy they had teaching it was okay. He was into his subject and that was pretty much all he cared about. If you did your work then he left you alone, which was fine by me. We were studying World War II, and our assignment was to research something that interested us about Canada's involvement in the war. I'd chosen the fall of Hong Kong: my dad's dad had been there with the Royal Rifles of Canada and had been captured by the Japanese. I only knew this because Mom had given me an old military badge and some shoulder flashes when Dad died, telling me that they were the only things he'd never tried to hock. I still have them, hidden in the lining of my coat along with that photo of Jon. I was pretty much ahead on my work, so I snuck out the copy I'd made of the Mueller family tree.

I noticed that Katerina Mueller had gotten married in 1891, the year after her brother Jacob's death. She'd married a man called Ephraim Sparrow and they had three children in pretty rapid succession. I felt like a dork. The fact that she had been married had never occurred to me. I would have continued pounding away at the Mueller name and come up with nothing at all, but now I wondered: Was our Jacob a relative of hers at all? The Mueller name had died out in this family. But the coincidence of brothers called Jacob and Caspar seemed odd.

It was while I was pondering this and tracing my finger down the twisting lines of Katerina's children's children, trying to arrive at the present day, that I got the awful feeling that someone was looking over my shoulder. He'd come up on the side of my bad eye. Mr. Halloran. He didn't make a huge deal out of it—I wasn't a kid who normally goofed off—just pulled the paper out from under my hand and walked away, telling me to get back to what I should have been doing.

I stewed for the remaining ten minutes of class, hating the fact that I was going to have to ask for the family tree back, maybe explain why I was looking at it.

Halloran had the sheet on his desk when I slouched up to him at the end of the lesson, waiting until everyone else had left the room.

"Homework for other subjects I'm used to, comic books, porn, maybe even a novel for the more erudite of my students, but I've never seen anyone looking at a family tree instead of working." Halloran was smiling as he spoke. "I suppose I should be glad, Mike, that it has some historical connection. Is it your family?"

I stopped myself from blurting out "no." I needed to get him off my back, so it seemed easier to say it was. "My dad's family. I found it when I was looking up stuff on the Internet about my granddad for the project. His mother was a Sparrow." I pointed vaguely at what I thought was the right time period for it to be true.

Halloran looked up at me, studying my face as if he were trying to gauge how truthful I was being. "The Sparrows were quite a well-known family in the area. They had one of the first farms down near what's now the east end." That meant nothing to me. Until I got sent to Medlar House, I'd never been to Hamilton before. "Barton Street," he added, "down near the lake, where the steel mills are now."

Those I knew. I'd seen them from the highway— huge smoke stacks billowing flame—when the social worker first drove me to Medlar.

"Are you going to research this further?" There was a pathetic gleam of hope in his eye. I knew what he was thinking; he thought he'd found that one student that all teachers dream about, the one who shares their love of their subject. "Maybe your family could help you."

Oh yes, my cunning brain was working and I saw a way to turn all of this to my advantage. I looked down, avoided his eyes, and said, "I'd like to, but I'm not with my family anymore." I hesitated here, hoping he would think that I was struggling not to lose it. "I'm one of the kids from the group home." He'd probably been told this at some point and it had slipped his mind, but I wasn't ashamed to make him squirm a little. "It's not easy to get computer time, or to the library. The other kids give you a hard time if they think you're a keener when it comes to school. That's why I was looking at it in class. I'm kind of as far along as I can be with my assignment until I find a way to do some more research." I allowed myself a quick look at his face, to see if he was buying it.

It had worked. Halloran was one of those guys with really pale skin, and he had gone red with embarrassment, probably as a result of my mentioning my family situation. He cleared his throat and said, "Look, Mike, I can't do anything about the library, but if you don't abuse it—by this I mean tell your friends and have them all pile in thinking they can play games—I don't see why you couldn't come into my classroom at lunchtime and use the computer here." He paused, giving me a little smile. "That way you can give your work your full attention during class, right?"

Score! I looked appropriately hangdog and grateful, shuffling my feet. "I won't. You don't know how much this means to me, Mr. Halloran." I couldn't resist turning the knife a little. "Most teachers think we're a bunch of thugs—the kids from the group home, I mean."

I thought that was a good touch. After all, was I not the thug of thugs when I wanted to be? I was already planning what use I could put this unexpected computer access to next week.

I'd almost made it through the door when Halloran called out, "Mike, I've just thought of something."

I turned around, but I wasn't going back in.

"The local collection and archives at the central library. I'm sure you'll find stuff on the Sparrow family there."

He'd gotten my attention. "Can I search it from the computer?"

"Afraid not. It's on the third floor, tucked away at the back. Everything is on a card index, but if you look up Sparrow, they'll have all sorts of stuff."

Damn, I thought. I'd have to find a way to get there somehow.

Chaz was late coming to get us that day. We waited where we always did out in front of the school, in our usual untidy knot. Surprisingly, today Matt was in the middle of the crowd and Paddy stood alone. Paddy kept up his sly grin, though, which pissed me off, but what could I do?

The cold that had almost done Jacob in yesterday had intensified. A few snowflakes drifted down. Gradually the parking lot emptied. The last bus pulled out, and we were the only ones there. I glanced around quickly, making sure that no one was watching and no one was coming through the main doors. I launched myself away from the wall, slamming into Paddy, one arm tight around his neck. To a casual observer, it would have looked innocent enough: two teenage boys roughhousing. Paddy tried to shake free of me, but I held him tight. I was amused that Matt made no effort to come to his friend's aid. Paddy tore at my arm with his hands, fighting to get free. Lowering my head, so that it was close to his, I whispered, "You know that I know that you did it. What you don't know is what I am going to do to you, and when it will be. Live in fear!" Okay, that last bit was over the top.

I heard the chugging wheeze of Chaz's van coming up the driveway and released my grip on Paddy's neck, taking a step back to distance myself from him a bit. Paddy sprang toward me, swinging his backpack at my head. It was beautiful. All Chaz saw was me standing there, hands in my pockets, and Paddy attacking me. You'd almost think I'd planned that. I sat back and enjoyed the harangue Paddy got about fighting. As he got on the bus last, Paddy mouthed "Adam!" to me and drew his finger across his throat.

At dinner, Chaz tried to pump me for information. Had I seen anything? Had anyone been talking about who had attacked Jacob? What had caused Paddy to take a swing at me? I could honestly tell him that I'd neither seen nor heard anything useful.

He sighed. It amazed me that someone like Chaz could be so innocent and optimistic after all that he must have seen. I almost felt guilty for what I was about to do.

We'd been silent for a while. "Chaz," I said, "I need to ask you something."

Okay, it was the first time I had ever initiated a conversation with him, but even so his reaction was extreme. He blinked, his mouth hung open, a forkful of food suspended in front of it, and the sad thing was that I could see the hope in his goddamned eyes.

"In history, we're doing a project on World War II, and my teacher told me that some of the information I need might be in the local collection at the central library. Do you think I could go and check it out?"

You could tell he was disappointed, but too bad. What was he thinking, that I was going to say, "Oooh, Chaz, let me tell you my innermost thoughts so I can exorcize the demons that plague me because of my brother's murder and the rest of my shitty life and everything will be all right from now on"?

"Yeah, that can be arranged," he said, his voice flat and tired-sounding now. "It's Saturday tomorrow.

I'm not officially on duty, but I'm going to pick Luce and Jacob up and bring them home." He winced as he said that last word, as conscious as I was that this was the last place you would want to think of as home. "I could swing by here and pick you up, if it's okay with whoever is in charge tomorrow, then run you down there, do some errands, and come back for you before I go to the hospital. How much time do you need?"

I had no idea. "An hour, maybe two. Mr. Halloran says that none of it is computerized so it might take me a while to find what I'm looking for."

"Let's split the difference, make it an hour and a half. I'll be here at 9:30."

It was all too easy. Looking back now, I wish it hadn't been, because if I hadn't gone to the library and found that stuff, then I wouldn't be up to my ears in shit now.

Chapter Eight

I was waiting at the door when Chaz arrived the next morning. I'd gone to my room immediately after dinner the night before and stayed there. Adam had given me a plaintive look, but Chaz was on duty for part of the night so I knew he'd be okay. I had a lot to think about, and I wanted to run through everything I knew about Jacob and try to come up with a story that hung together. I didn't succeed, just gave myself a headache.

In places like these, the weekends are the worst. There is nothing to do. For a few unlucky people there are visitors. There are always more arguments, mainly out of boredom. So, you can imagine it didn't sit well with the kids who had overheard my conversation with Chaz last night that I was getting to go out, even if it was to the library.

Adam had been waiting outside my room again that morning. He didn't bother with any small talk, just greeted me by stating baldly, "You have to take me. Paddy will get me if you don't. He said he knew I'd told." His face was white and pinched, the bruises around his eye even more noticeable today.

Shit. I hadn't exactly forgotten about him, but I was just too hung up on the possibility of finally finding Jacob's family. "I don't know, buddy. I'm just going to the library; it'll be boring as hell."

His upper lip started to quiver and the finger-twisting started up again.

"Look, I'll ask Chaz. It'll be up to him, okay?" God, I was getting soft.

Adam didn't leave my side all through breakfast, even managing to finagle himself into Jacob's usual place. I concentrated on my breakfast, but whenever I looked up, he was giving me puppy dog eyes.

Paddy was waiting in the hall when Adam and I came out of the dining room, leaning against the wall nearest the common room. Matt was nowhere in sight. Maybe I had succeeded in frightening him away with my antics outside the school yesterday.

At first Paddy said nothing, just stood there staring at me. Then he started making wet kissing noises. I could see a few curious faces peering out of the common room, eyes round with anticipation. A couple of kids giggled, which spurred him on. He opened his mouth and let his tongue flicker back and forth suggestively.

The giggling rose in volume.

"So what are we talking about here? Butt boys together?" Paddy's voice was low, but loud enough so that everyone could hear.

I didn't answer.

"I mean, that must be the explanation." Paddy looked around at his audience before continuing. "Why you're so concerned about Jacob, and, of course, why Chaz is always willing to help you out. Although I would have thought that face of yours would turn most people off. What are you going to do for him in return, Mike?" He did an exaggerated double take when he saw Adam next to me, clutching his coat. "Maybe he likes them young, younger than you. I'm getting a bit of a pedo vibe here. Are you his supplier?"

I felt anger rising in me, a wash of hate that would only be stopped when I pounded the smirk off Paddy's face. I was stepping toward him, fist raised, when I felt a tug on my sleeve. Adam was there, shaking his head. He nodded toward Paddy, who was moving forward, clearly not preparing to defend himself, just smiling and almost offering his face to be hit. I shuddered with the realization of how close he had come to making me blow my chance to get to the library. I shook myself free of Adam's grasp roughly, gave him the slightest nod, and stepped back. Lowering my arm, I turned my attention back to the door. I made myself give him a smile and muttered, "Nice try, Paddy. It almost worked."

He snarled something I didn't catch and then I heard the thump of a fist and a squeal as he took out his frustration on someone else. Since I could see Chaz was pulling up outside, I didn't bother to turn around to find out how or on whom.

Chaz looked a bit better than he had the day before. He raised his eyebrows when he saw Adam standing next to me, his coat on, looking hopeful. I thought on my feet and came up with some hokey story about Adam having homework that needed research in the library, too, adding that I would look after him. I could almost see the questions forming in Chaz's mind. I was willing to bet that the first would be: When had Adam and I started to talk to each other? If he was as smart as I thought he was, then Chaz would try and find some way to make use of this information. In the end, he just shrugged. After all, Adam was one of the good kids, one of the ones who rarely caused trouble.

Saturday was obviously a big day downtown; the library was way busier than it had been during my weekday visit. I was never one for crowds, even before, but now I outright hate them. I am always conscious of the stares, the quick aversion of eyes, and the whispers. I was glad when we reached the local collection.

Following Mr. Halloran's directions, it was easy to find. Best of all, the librarians outnumbered the visitors there. There were maybe three other people in the room, all sitting quietly at their tables. Only one looked up when we came in, and he dropped his gaze back to whatever he was reading in a matter of seconds. Adam stuck close to me, almost tripping on my heels. He started to tell me that the library was a place he used to go to a lot with his mother, because it was free. I told him to can it, that I wasn't interested.

It was like stepping back in time. I'm sure this is how libraries looked before computers. It was just a big room with huge wooden tables. At one end there were racks of what looked like file folders, at the other a bank of wooden card-catalog boxes.

Adam's eyes widened. "Where are the computers?" he asked.

I pointed to the card catalogs. "There's cards in there, in alphabetical order." I'd brought a pad and pencil with me; now I tore off a piece of paper and gave it to him. There were stubby pencils sitting on top of the catalogs so I got him one of those, too, telling him to go look for anything on Sparrow, particularly Katerina. I tried looking up Jacob Mueller first of all, but there was nothing. Just as I was looking for Caspar, I heard a whoop from Adam. It was so quiet in there that everyone turned to stare at him; the librarian just smiled and put a finger to her lips.

He turned scarlet, but he waved me over, looking very pleased with himself.

He had found a card for the Sparrow family; apparently, it referred to a newspaper article from a 1975 issue of *The Spectator*. There was also a separate catalog entry for Katerina Sparrow, and this was odd: it listed her as the author of a pamphlet printed in 1890 called "The Prophet."

I'll admit it. I'm a computer guy through and through. I had no idea how to get hold of the stuff that was listed on the cards. The librarian at the desk was good. She looked me straight in the eye, no flinching, and explained what I needed to do. The newspaper article was the easier of the two to access. I just had to write down the volume number and page, and I could find it myself in the folders at the back of the room. As for the pamphlet, the original was available if I wanted to apply for an archive card, or they had a photocopy of it. For that, I just had to fill out a form and they would bring it to me at one of the tables. She also said that I could photocopy it myself if I wanted to. There was a machine for this behind the card boxes. To say I was excited would have been an understatement. Adam was still pumped about being the one to find the Sparrow family card. I think our enthusiasm tickled the librarian.

We found an unoccupied table and sat down, Adam hovering as close to me as possible so he could read over my shoulder. I whispered to him to explain what I was looking for and he nodded sagely, as if this was the most logical thing he had ever heard. The article was part of a series on local history that had been published over the years in *The Spectator*. From it, we learned that the Sparrows had settled in Head of the Lake, which was what Hamilton was known as in the early part of the nineteenth century. They were loyalists who'd sided with the British in the Revolutionary War and were chased out of America, north to Canada, at the end of the war. There was even a Sparrow Street named after them, but the name had died out in the area. Ephraim Sparrow and Katerina had only had daughters, one of whom never married. The other had married a man from Waterloo County and moved there with him. That sucked big time. I'd hit another dead end, unless Jacob might possibly be a descendant of that daughter, but then why would he have the surname Mueller? The only explanation I could come up with was that perhaps he was trying to hide his real identity. Waterloo County was near Kitchener, not that far away, but it all seemed flimsy and unlikely.

I was wondering what to do next when Adam whispered to me, "It's Katerina who is important." He was definitely a smart cookie; as I thought about it, it struck me that he was probably right. And he obviously read faster than I did because he suddenly pointed further down the article and there it was!

Katerina was described as a colorful character who'd spent her early years traveling with and looking after her brother, Jacob Mueller, who was known locally as The Prophet, their capitals not mine. So, maybe, just maybe, the name Jacob Mueller was one that had been passed down and made a big deal of in the Sparrow family.

I was curious about this Prophet and am a sucker for that kind of weird stuff, so even though it probably wasn't going to lead anywhere, I asked for the photocopy of the pamphlet. The clock on the wall told me that we had a while before Chaz would arrive, or so I thought. The librarian had just delivered the pamphlet when he was there, looming over my shoulder.

"Dry and dusty, Mike." He sounded amused. "You never stop surprising me. Are you ready to go? What about you, Adam?"

Adam waved the piece of paper I'd given him, and I was tickled to see that he had taken the time to write stuff down. "Yes, I got what I need." Thankfully, Chaz was not the sort to examine things closely.

I was beginning to genuinely like this kid; he was smart and he thought on his feet.

I hesitated. "I need this for my history project," I said to Chaz. "They said I could photocopy it . . ." I hoped he would take the bait. He didn't disappoint me.

Chaz reached into his pocket and pulled out a crumpled ten-dollar bill. "See if they can change that. Quick, though, because Luce called to say that they're doing the paperwork to release Jacob and they should be ready to go in about half an hour."

The pamphlet was thin, no more than ten pages of cramped old-fashioned type, with an illustration at the end, one of those old-school line drawings that were used in newspapers and stuff before photographs. I didn't have time to examine it closely, but it was pretty obvious that something was missing from the original: the last page seemed to end in a jagged tear. I copied the newspaper article, too, just in case I had missed something. I carefully put the photocopied sheets inside my notebook, gave the items back to the librarian, and we were off.

True to form, Chaz had parked in the loading area, and we rushed to the van, oblivious to the glares we were getting from a truck driver waiting to unload produce for the market.

I don't know what I was expecting when we got to the hospital, but the sight of Jacob hunched up in a wheelchair scared me. He looked smaller and thinner, lost in the blanket wrapped around him. He was staring straight ahead, but didn't seem to register anything when the van pulled to a halt and Luce wheeled him toward it. He was a mess. Livid bruises, still freshly purple, blotched his skin. The left side of his face was a scabbed-over graze. Lucy didn't look much better. She was pale and had dark circles under her eyes as if she hadn't slept well, which was probably the case if my memory of nights in the hospital were anything to go by.

Chaz leaped down from the van and bent over Jacob, talking softly to him but getting no response. Jacob continued to stare into space, and it seemed like he was hardly blinking.

Straightening up, Chaz said, "Lucy, are you sure they should be releasing him?" That's what I was thinking, too.

Lucy looked close to tears. "There's nothing physically wrong with him that won't heal." She looked down at Jacob, patted his shoulder. "He's eating, well, as much as he ever does. Believe it or not, he seemed to like the hospital food, all those separate bowls and packets, simple food. He even talked to one of the doctors once, told him his name and his age, but every so often he gets like this, like he isn't here, and nothing anyone does can change that. We just have to wait for him."

Chaz hugged Lucy, patting her back like you would with a child. "He's been through a tough time, Luce. You know what he's like when things get to be too much for him. Once we get him back to Medlar House, familiar surroundings, I'll bet that he'll do this less and less." It sounded like Chaz was trying to convince himself; his voice lacked its usual confidence. He paused. "What about school? The principal called me yesterday, supposedly to ask about Jacob, but really the bastard was just covering his own back. He gave me a whole load of crap about how this wouldn't have happened if Jacob had gone to class like he was supposed to, as if he even knows if Jacob was bunking off or if those thugs grabbed him when he was on his way to class."

"No problem there," answered Luce. "He's not allowed to go back until he's been cleared by the pediatrician here, and they set up an appointment with him for ten days from now."

I hadn't realized that I had been holding my breath, but these words from Lucy let me breathe again with relief. Jacob was safe. He'd be at Medlar House with whoever was on duty, and I would be there to watch over him, making sure that Paddy didn't try anything.

Lucy unwrapped the blanket and Chaz leaned down and picked Jacob up. Chaz was a big rangy guy, but still, it seemed like it took no effort at all. He carried Jacob easily up the steps of the van and buckled him into the seat across the aisle from mine. I tried to catch his eye, but Jacob just kept staring straight ahead. When the van rumbled into life, he shuddered, then shut his eyes.

Jacob was back with us.

I don't know what I was expecting, exactly. Jacob had talked to me, but only when no one else was around. So it was hardly likely that he'd do it now, but it didn't stop me hoping. I watched him all the way back, responding to Lucy with no more than grunts when she tried to make conversation about what I'd found in the library for my supposed history project. She gave up and turned her attention to Adam.

Boy, was he good. He conjured up this whole story about a geography project on where he lived and was going into all this detail about how I'd helped him figure out how to find historical information about the street Medlar House sat on. He gave me a sly smile and added, "The family that lived there when it was first built was called Sparrow."

I gave him a warning look and he slid down into his seat.

Chaz hadn't exactly glared at me when I gave Lucy the silent treatment but he hadn't looked pleased, either. I wanted to stay in his good books, so as soon as we pulled into the drive in front of Medlar House, I was out the door first. I stood there holding the front door open as Chaz exited the van carrying Jacob, followed by Lucy and Adam. Chaz ignored the gawkers who, sensing that something unusual was happening, appeared miraculously out of thin air, and headed straight up the stairs toward our room. Lucy started trying to herd everyone else back to whatever it was they'd been doing. Me, I just followed Chaz. After all, it was my room, too, and maybe once I'd got rid of Chaz, Jacob would talk to me again. Yeah,

I wanted him to confirm what Adam had told me about who'd beaten the shit out of him, but more importantly, I now really believed he spoke to the dead. I'd heard them. I wanted him to do it again.

Still in polite-and-helpful-boy mode, I managed to maneuver myself ahead of Chaz and open the door to our room. When I started to follow him in, though, he stopped in the doorway.

"Not so fast, big boy." He looked down at Jacob, who, with his shut eyes, gave every appearance of being asleep. "Let him have some space. I know you found him, but it's not like you're great buddies, is it?"

What could I say? If I told Chaz that the reason I wanted to hang out with Jacob was so I could talk to my dead brother, he would have wasted no time rushing me off to the nut house.

I didn't argue. There was no point. I could wait until night.

Like I said, the weekends are shit awful in places like Medlar House. It was lunchtime, more chaotic than usual because we were being supervised by Bob and this other guy, Larry. Lucy had gone home and Chaz was sitting on the landing outside our room, making sure that Jacob was left alone. All I wanted was to be alone so I could look at the pamphlet I'd photocopied. Without my room as an option, I thought I might have to knock a few heads to find a quiet place to read by myself. Luck was on my side.

Since Chaz was staying, which was weird because he'd said that he wasn't on duty, Larry suggested that he and Bob take everyone down to the public pool for a swim, and anyone who didn't want to go could stay with Chaz. Bob looked sour at the idea but gave in. Oh, the screaming this provoked, the rushing around looking for swimsuits and towels. When the dust settled, everyone but me, Adam, and, surprisingly, Matt was gone.

I figured I had two hours of peace.

Matt and Adam were in the common room, watching some old movie, when I went in. I thought about turfing Matt out, but the look of fear in his eyes when I grinned at him menacingly convinced me that he wouldn't give me any trouble. And Adam seemed quite comfortable with him, which surprised me. Maybe all the shit he had taken had come from Paddy alone. Matt must have stood by and done nothing to stop it, though, so he wasn't exactly a good guy, but maybe Adam was just the forgiving type.

I sat down at a table by the window. My bad eye aches if I try to read in anything but good light. I knew that the tiny print was going to be murder to read, but I wanted to find out just who this Prophet was.

Adam looked up from the screen and mimed coming over, but I shook my head and was surprised when he didn't protest, just settled back down on the sofa and said something to Matt that made him smile.

I'd given up on the idea that this pamphlet would be any help in finding out who Jacob really was. It was coincidence, nothing more, that this woman had brothers whose names were the same as Jacob and his brother, Caspar.

Now, if you think I like big words, you'd be blown away by old Katerina Mueller/Sparrow, because she used the longest, most obscure words I've ever come across. The pamphlet's opening sentence set the tone:

"Although of late, I have been a sojourner in darkness, I scribe here on what was the golden time of my tatterdemalion existence: the time I was companion and amanuensis to my brother Jacob Mueller, late of Dundas, known to all as The Prophet."

I'm pretty smart, but some of the words she used stumped me completely. It didn't really matter; I was able to tease out the gist of what she was saying. She and her brothers had been born on a farm somewhere near St. Jacobs—or Jakobstettel, as it was known then—but they were only her half brothers and were older than her by quite a bit. They were born in 1850 and 1852, and she had been born in 1862. It got confusing then, because she suddenly went all coy, hinting at some great evil, an "unnatural act" that happened when she was three, without ever explaining what it was, only that she and her oldest brother, Jacob, had to flee for their lives. There was a whole passage here about the innocent saved from a cruel fate. I presumed she was talking about herself, but it wasn't really clear. Jacob seemed to have been her original savior, but afterward, she was in the care of *"those who had nurtured and raised my poor, dead mother,"* and Jacob had *"vanished from the face of the earth and the knowledge of all its denizens for a period of months, which led those who cared for him to believe him in heaven with the angels."*

I really was getting a headache now, but old Katerina managed to hold my attention, especially when Jacob mysteriously reappeared, then lived with her and her mother's relatives until he was old enough to *"peregrinate through the highways and byways making use of his God-given gifts to bring solace by esoteric and arcane means to those in mourning for lost loved ones, through messages and also by drawing likenesses of the departed so accurate that they made those who saw them weep. He also shared knowledge of wonders yet to come, thus earning the sobriquet of The Prophet."* Katerina seemed to have traveled with him, and it sounded like they made a living doing some kind of show in barns and halls wherever they ended up. She was obviously happy then, because she stated that she had no need of *"a child of my own flesh, finding fulfillment in acting as helpmeet to my brother, who paid the price for his gifts by receiving wariness and fear from the very ones whom he helped, living a lonely life bereft of companion-ship save that of his devoted sister."*

They seem to have done this for some years, until her Jacob died of an ague he contracted when they were caught in a snowstorm as they returned to their home in Dundas one winter. She finished by writing that although she had settled into the life of a wife and mother with Mr. Ephraim Sparrow of Hamilton, she still thought fondly of the days when she and Jacob had wandered freely, *"my life tinctured with the grace of the glorious unknown, and I hope that by selling this pamphlet, I would not only preserve the memory and knowledge of my dear brother but would also raise sufficient monies to build a lasting monument to mark the place where he settled."*

There was an appendix entitled "Wonders Yet to Come as Foreseen by The Prophet, Jacob Mueller," but all that was there was one line about how there would be boxes containing images of people who moved and spoke. Then there was the tear, so I guessed that there had been a few more wonders. After all, one predic-tion wouldn't have exactly inspired confidence in his prophetic abilities.

By the time I finished the pamphlet, my head ached worse than ever, but that wasn't the cause of my shaking hands or the cold sweat that was now running down my face. What freaked me out, made the hair at the back of my neck stand up, was the line drawing just before the appendix, which claimed to be *"a veritable likeness of The Prophet, Jacob Mueller, in the Halcyon Days of his Youth."*

If you aged him a few years, it was the spitting image of the Jacob Mueller who was lying asleep in our room upstairs. I must have gasped out loud—the likeness was so uncanny—because it brought Adam to my side. Matt looked quizzically at us from across the room.

"That's Jacob, only older! We found something," Adam whispered, almost hopping up and down with glee. "This must be his family. When we read the article it said that one of his sister's daughters moved away. You need to find her children, Mike—they are probably the ones who drew up the tree!" I couldn't help smiling at his enthusiasm, but I didn't have time to think about how I was going to achieve this, because just then the swimming party burst in. Paddy started flicking Matt viciously with his wet towel until he squealed in pain. Seeing Adam standing by me at the table, Paddy grimaced and once again mimed cutting his throat. The joy in Adam's face evaporated and his shoulders hunched as he inched closer to my side.

Chapter Nine

That night, Jacob surprised me. Helped by Chaz, he limped down for dinner, taking his usual seat opposite me. Like the morning before his beating, he kept sneaking glances at me when he thought I wasn't looking. Only I was *always* looking. Finally, he realized that I was watching him as closely as he was watching me, and as he ducked his head in a strange little nod, I could have sworn he smiled. Chaz, who seemed dead on his feet, was oblivious to this byplay, and concentrated entirely on making sure that Jacob ate something.

After the meal ended, I was on clean-up duty with Matt, who was the exact opposite of Jacob in that he was doing everything he could to avoid eye contact with me. I couldn't resist. When he was scraping stuff into the compost bin, I crept up behind him and tapped his shoulder. He leaped about three feet in the air, then shrieked when he saw me there.

"Don't hit me!" His face contorted in fear.

I gave him my best feral grin. "Now why would I want to do that, Matt?"

Backing away, he nearly tripped over the bin, righting himself only by clutching at the wall. He was sweating and his eyes flickered from side to side, looking for a way out or for rescue in the form of someone else coming into the kitchen. "It wasn't my idea." He was stuttering and breathless, desperate to exonerate himself. "It was Paddy. He said it would be a laugh, and got some other kids involved, the ones who always like to give the kids from here grief."

This was better than I'd hoped. I didn't say anything, just continued to stare at him.

It did the trick. The words came tumbling out. "They jumped Jacob at recess, dragged him to the bleachers." Matt shuddered, swallowed hard. "He didn't even try to fight them off. He just lay there, like he was dead." Tears were coming now, and he struggled to speak. "Mike, you gotta believe me, I didn't do anything. I couldn't. I watched is all, and I wish I hadn't. I wish I hadn't. Fuck, I wish I hadn't been there at all, because then I wouldn't have heard them." Matt looked like he was going to throw up. "The others didn't hear anything. I know—if they had, they would have stopped and they would have run, too. It was voices, Mike, I heard voices whispering from the shadows."

It was a struggle to keep anything from showing on my face, but I managed it, fighting down the exultation inside me. Matt had heard something under the bleachers, too. I wasn't a complete nutjob.

Matt slid down the wall, sitting with his legs drawn up to his chest. He wasn't looking at me anymore. He had his head down on his knees and although his voice was muffled, the words indistinct and clotted with snot, I could still hear him. "Most of them, they didn't matter, some weren't even talking English, but I heard my gran's voice, Mike. She was crying and she kept saying my name. Then she was going, 'Don't let them do this, Matt. It's not right. I raised you better.'" He looked up at me then, his eyes big with tears and fear. "I felt her hand on my shoulder, the way she used to rest it there. I ran then, Mike. I ran like hell because my gran's dead. She's been dead for two years, which is why I'm in this shithole."

I didn't say anything, just reached down, grabbed Matt's arm, and hauled him to his feet. He flinched away and I could feel how much he was shaking. Dropping his arm, I grabbed some paper towels and handed them to him, then turned to leave the kitchen.

I had to leave before my anger blasted its way out. How come Matt's ghost talked to him? Jacob had said that Jon spoke to him. Why couldn't I hear him, if I had been able to hear the other voices? I was almost out of the room when Matt spoke again. "Shit, you heard them, too, didn't you, when you found him? Which of those voices was speaking to you?"

That did it. I turned and ran back, ramming him hard against the wall. I grabbed his shirt tight in one hand and twisted it up. "What are you, some kind of weirdo? Voices? What fucking voices? You're sick!"

Matt didn't say anything, didn't even struggle, just kept looking at me. Nothing I was doing was convincing him that he was wrong, that I hadn't heard the voices, too. Only he didn't know it all. He didn't know that I *wanted* to hear them. There was one voice I needed to hear, but it wasn't speaking to me. That's why I needed to talk to Jacob. With one last shove, I let go.

Chaz was in the hallway, shrugging on his coat, car keys in hand. "Mike, Jacob's asleep. Try not to wake him up when you go to bed." I nodded, even though I was set on doing exactly that. "Keep an eye on him. No heroics: get a staff member if you think something is wrong."

"Okay," I answered. I didn't want to waste any more time, just get up there and find out what was going on.

Chaz gave me a weary smile. "Mike," he said, "man of few words—only, I'm beginning to think it's all a bit of an act." He put on this obviously fake, syrupy voice, sounding like one of those greasy game show hosts announcing the crap prizes. "Beneath that rough, tough exterior beats a heart of gold."

Whatever. I turned and walked up the stairs.

Asleep, my ass!

I'll give Jacob credit. It was passable. He was lying on his back like he usually did. He was doing the regular, gentle breathing thing, but if you looked closely you could see that his eyes weren't completely shut; he was looking at me through his eyelashes.

"Chaz has gone," I said.

There was no response at first. Then Jacob slowly sat up, the pain from his bruises obvious on his face with each movement. He put one finger to his lips and pointed with his other hand to the clock on the bedside table, tracing a circle twice, then nodding.

Later, he meant. Two hours would take us to lights-out. I refused to let him see how much the wait bothered me and nonchalantly got out a book and pretended to read it, but really I was watching Jacob. He lay on his bed, staring at the ceiling. Every so often he scrunched up his face as if he was trying to remember something, or trying to pass a particularly big turd.

When the call for lights-out came, I quickly went to the bathroom and by the time I came back Jacob had rolled over onto his side so that he was facing my bed. I flicked the bedside lamp off and waited, listening to the sounds outside die away until all I could hear was a muted television.

"Mutt," I heard. That papery voice creeped me out. Who was this speaking to me? "Mutt, he said you would come. Jon said you would save me."

My heart felt like lead—it was Jacob talking.

I couldn't help it: the words burst out of me. I sounded like a whiny little kid. "You said that Jon had gone away, that I couldn't talk to him! That was a fucking lie."

"He did go, but he came back because he is my friend and I was in danger. If he came, then he knew that you'd come to help me." I heard the rustle of bedclothes and saw the gleam of Jacob's eyes as he turned to face me. "Jon knows you did not let him down. He knows you tried to protect him. You must believe that. No one is to blame but Danny. That's the truth and nothing will change it." He sighed and his voice was sad. "I do not know why, but it is hard for our own dead to talk directly to us. Perhaps the connection is too strong. They fear we will beg them to stay and then they will be powerless. I see and hear everyone else's ghosts so clearly, but never my own. It's part of me, like breathing. There are others like you and that boy Matt, who can hear them in times of great danger or great feeling, but it does not last." His expression was dejected as he added, "Me, I have no choice but to hear them—I don't know if I should be glad or if I am cursed, like my foda says."

I wanted to cry. Jacob reached out a hand, hesitantly, like I might lash out at him, and touched my sleeve. "Jon must go. His pull to you is too strong. You loved him so much. He knows that in time, you will believe what he says. The knowledge is there in your heart, but you deny it."

I shivered. Did I dare believe what Jacob was telling me? That it wasn't my fault? It would be so easy to do that.

Jacob's face crinkled up like he was going to cry. "I loved my brother, my Caspar, as much as you loved Jon. I wish he had known that I was on my way back to him. I would have fought for him, even though Foda is a man and I'm just a boy. Didn't I fight back when he hit little Kat? Caspar did, too—we held Foda back so she could run from the dairy." He started to sob. "Foda killed Caspar and I could do nothing. I was not back in time. I felt the blows. I bled with him. I ran away when the killing blow came."

I was so lost in my own reverie that at first I didn't respond to his words. Finally I registered that Jacob was actually talking, and not just talking a little; now he wouldn't shut up. The mention of Caspar and Kat made me sit up and take notice. This was serious shit. If I'd got it right, this Foda (his father, maybe?) had hit his sister and then killed his brother, and Jacob had run away after being beaten himself. Could this be right? Surely something like that couldn't be hidden, but if no one had come looking for Jacob, maybe it had.

"Jacob," I said, keeping my voice as quiet as I could. "Are you saying your brother is dead? That someone called Foda killed him?"

His sobs broke off and he lifted his head. Almost impatiently, he said, "Yes, yes, that is what I said."

You know how the hair along a dog's spine stands up when the dog feels threatened or scared? Well, I had that feeling then, that something was about to happen and that it wasn't going to be good.

Jacob had gotten into a loop now talking about Caspar, and I heard him mention Kat a few more times, too. He kept talking about being in the other place and how he needed to tell Caspar that he had been coming back for him, but he had not been fast enough. Over and over he said this, not making any sense.

It got to me. "Jacob," I said. "Jacob, listen to me. I want to show you something. Maybe it will help lead us to your Foda guy. Maybe we can tell someone about Caspar and what Foda did to him?" God, I realize now how dense and obtuse I was being here.

Jacob was having none of it, though; he had curled up, hands around his knees, and was rocking back and forth as he muttered to himself.

In desperation, I turned the bedside lamp on. "Jacob!" I whispered forcefully. I couldn't shout because I didn't want whoever was on duty to come running. "Shut the fuck up!"

Whether it was the sudden light or the urgency in my voice I don't know, but it worked. Jacob slowly straightened out his body and stared at me, his mouth hanging open in surprise.

I heard something then—a rustle outside our door. Shit, I must have been louder than I thought. The last thing I wanted was Bob or Larry coming in to see why we were still awake. I put my finger to my lips—not that I thought Jacob was about to speak, but I wanted the element of surprise—and pulled the door open.

Adam. He was sitting cross-legged, hunched up against our door like a little rock. I grabbed his arm and hauled him inside, closing the door quietly.

"What the fuck are you doing here again? Don't give me the 'I'm frightened of Paddy' crap. He wouldn't try anything with your roommate there."

Adam didn't say anything, just started to cry. He made no sound, but I could see tears rolling down his cheeks.

I sighed, wondering how long he'd been out there and how much he'd heard. "Look, just get out of here, okay? This doesn't concern you." I was frustrated because I thought that I might have been getting somewhere with Jacob. "I'll watch and make sure you get back to your room."

Between sniffles, Adam whispered, "I wanted to be here when you told Jacob what we found."

No. I wasn't having that. "Come on, get going," I insisted. When Adam didn't move I pushed him toward the door. I was gentle about it, but I really didn't want him in our room just then.

"No!"

Both Adam and I stopped in our tracks. Adam was surprised, I think, because he had never heard Jacob speak. Me, I just couldn't get my head around why Jacob might want Adam to stay.

"He helped you, yes?" Jacob was leaning forward now, sitting on the edge of his bed.

"Yeah, I guess," I admitted grudgingly.

"He should stay." There was determination in his voice. "He is one of the lost ones, too."

This was spooky. Who were the lost ones? Was I a lost one?

I felt Adam relax, and he took advantage of the pause to wriggle away from me and sit next to Jacob.

"I see her," Jacob said, as matter-of-factly as if he was talking about the weather. "She watches him and tells me about this boy. She is sad that she had to leave him. It wasn't planned. She loves him so much. Not since my own mutta has a mother loved her son so hard. Too hard."

Adam's eyes had widened. He grabbed Jacob's arm. I could see how hard he was gripping it. "Mummy. You see and talk to my mother?"

Jacob nodded. "She has told me how she always kept you safe. How scared she was that people would take you away from her. She said that perhaps this made her do some wrong things."

Adam's eyes were closed now. I hadn't really thought too much about his past before—mainly I was just irritated by his constant references to his mother—but there was obviously a hell of a story there. Still, I didn't want to hear it now.

"Enough!" I said, my voice harsher than I had intended. "You can stay, Adam. Jacob, you were talking about Caspar and Kat . . ."

Jacob seemed to be in as much of a daydream as Adam. My words weren't getting through, so I thrust the last page of the pamphlet at him. His eyes grew wide as he stared at it. When he spoke, his voice cracked. "This is me, but I am old. Why did you draw a picture of me like this?"

"No, no, I didn't draw it, Jacob," I said, a bit exasperated. "I've been looking in the library for information, trying to find your family, to get you out of here if I can. This is an old pamphlet written by a woman called Katerina Mueller, about her brother who was called Jacob like you, and she had a brother Caspar, too. So, I thought these people must be related to you: the names are probably family ones used over and over again through the years, see?" I could tell from the mulish look on his face that he wasn't buying this at all.

Adam piped up. "We found this at the library this morning."

Still no reaction from Jacob, just the stubborn look on his face. I tried again. "She had daughters and one of them married a man from Kitchener." His face remained stony.

Adam interrupted "Kitchener used to be called Berlin. They changed the name during World War I."

That was news to me, but Adam was the kind of smart-ass who would know something like that.

Jacob stirred slightly, so I continued. "I found her married name, and maybe we can trace the rest of her family, her descendants, to see if they know who you are." I rested my hand on my forehead, not daring to look over to see if he was taking this in.

"Katerina is my sister, and Caspar was my brother," he whispered.

"No, goddamn it! Read it and you'll see. These people are dead. They died a hundred years ago!" It was cruel, but I had to get through to him. I flipped the pamphlet over so he could see the front cover and pushed it into his hands. He let it fall onto his lap. Shit, I'd forgotten how rudimentary his reading was.

"Okay," I said, grabbing it back, "I'll read it to you." I could see this was going to be a long night.

Jacob leaned forward again and shut his eyes.

I felt ridiculous. He didn't seem to be paying much attention to old Katerina Mueller's flowery beginning, but his eyes opened and he sat bolt upright when I got to the bit about where and when she and her brothers were born.

A wide smile, one that was happy, even euphoric, spread across his face. "Katerina *is* my sister and Caspar *was* my brother. I am Jacob Mueller, and I am fifteen years old. I was born in 1850 on the farm of my foda, near Jakobstettel." The smile vanished as quickly as it had come. His whole face crumpled in on itself and he began to cry in earnest. "Katerina is dead, too, like Caspar?" He looked straight at me, his eyes begging me to tell him otherwise.

I can't describe what I was feeling at that point. I was beyond weirded out. Adam's face mirrored my reaction. He had both hands up to his mouth like he was trying to stop himself from shouting out. His eyes were wide and shocked. He turned to me, but didn't say anything, just nodded as if to let me know he was thinking the same as me. People talk about how they have gut feelings. My gut was talking to me big time. It was like I had a big neon sign in my head that was flashing "1850!" The little things added up: Jacob's weird likes and dislikes, his fear of cars. Even though my rational mind said it could not be possible, there was something deep inside of me that said it could, and if it was, then I had found Jacob Mueller's missing family, only they hadn't been missing for three or four months; they had been missing for a century and a half!

I hesitated, skimming the newspaper article. "She died in 1925, Jacob, almost a hundred years ago. She was an old lady, in her sixties. She lived most of her life in Hamilton." I was looking for things to say, trying to ease the pain that was etched on his face. "People loved her and came out to her funeral . . ." My voice trailed away.

He was rocking back and forth again now, a look of horror on his face. "This book, it says that I am dead, too? This cannot be, because I am here, even if it is the other place. Ah, I lost Caspar in the real place; now I have lost little Kat, too. She was three. Now you tell me she grew up and lived for so many years and I was lost to her!"

I sensed that he was on the verge of tuning out, melting down—that it was all too much for him. I had to keep him with me somehow. In a sudden burst it came to me: if I could trust the pamphlet, then I could give him hope. I reached out to touch his shoulder, but he pulled away.

"Jacob, listen. You went back." I searched for a way to put it so that he would understand. "You left this other place and you went back to the real one. You saw your Kat grow up. You grew up, too. You lived with her and you traveled together until . . ." I tried to swallow that last word before he heard it.

Jacob's sobs had stopped and he was looking at me like I had offered him a lifeline, which I suppose

I had, in a way. "Kat wrote about your life together. She says that you disappeared for months, then came back, and that you lived with her and what I think was her mother's family."

Jacob's face lit up with hope. "Yes, yes, that was where I was taking her: to her mother's family, to make her safe from Foda. But . . ." He paused, the joy fading from his face. "I am still here, in the other place. How can I go back?" After a moment's pause, he continued, his voice different, buoyant. "You!" His face broadened into the biggest smile I had ever seen from him. "Jon said you would help me. You will get me back to the real place."

Shit.

I had no idea how this was going to happen, but I knew that I had to try my damnedest to find a way. Jon had said I would, and there was no way I could let him down, not again.

Chapter Ten

It was a hell of a long night.

Some key had turned inside Jacob, unlocking him. Don't get me wrong; I'm not saying that everything was suddenly normal. He wasn't talking a mile a minute, but he was talking, even if it sounded bizarre, what with his odd diction, slight accent, and habit of repeating himself if he thought I didn't understand him, which a lot of the time I didn't.

I mean, come on: a kid, and one who could talk to the dead, falling sideways through time? How much fucking sense did that make? There were so many questions and no goddamn answers. How, why, and what the hell could I do to get him back to his "real place"? That was the one thing he was adamant about, that I could somehow make this happen. None of the objections I raised would move him. Mutt had the answer to everything because Jon had told him so.

I tried getting details from him—believe me I tried. Adam tried, too, but he kept sneaking in questions about his mother. Jacob sidestepped those by insisting that Adam's mother was not here now. When Adam's lip started to quiver, Jacob told him that she would come back eventually, to tell Adam something he wanted to know. I wanted to know stuff, too. I wanted to know what Jacob remembered, but direct questions shut him down and prompted more weeping, silent tears now rather than sobs. All I could do was wait for him.

In the end, it was reading Katerina's pamphlet to him in its entirety that filled in some of the gaps. I didn't want to do it, because I was going to have to tell him about his own death, which was something I was having real trouble getting my head around. The way I look at it is that we start to die from the moment we are born, but we choose not to think about it. Yeah, if you've got some illness there may come a time when the doctors will tell you that you're going to die soon, but that's like a short period to know. Can you imagine knowing from the time you're fifteen that you are going to die when you are forty? What does that do to the way you think, the way you live your life? Would you be able to let a day go by without thinking about that? Hell, the more I thought about it, the more I didn't want to read him that thing at all because it was telling him how he lived his life, a life that had already happened, so it couldn't be changed, right?

He begged and he begged. What could I do?

When I finally agreed, he lay down on his back in bed, crossing his arms on his chest, eyes open this time. I motioned to Adam that he should come and sit by me. I had to perch on the edge of my bed, leaning forward, so that I could use the bedside lamp to see. I wanted Adam there so he could do some of the reading, and we took turns, switching places each time for the best light.

I started from the beginning again, and this time, there were little comments, exhalations, and grimaces from Jacob's side of the room. I waited for him to stop me to explain some of old Katerina's fancy vocab, but he didn't, just smiled and whispered, more to himself than me, "Even at three little Kat was clever, and she became a clever woman."

The mention of the farm was a trigger: now Jacob spoke up. I sat back and listened to the monologue that drifted out in fits and starts, not all of it making sense.

"I was firstborn. It was I who should have been the strong one, but the voices, always I heard the voices. Mutta, she said there were others in her family who heard them, too, and that I should listen to what they told me. Not Foda." At this, Jacob's face tightened. "Foda, he said it was the devil talking to me, and he beat me to drive the voices away. They learned and became clever, and after a while they never talked to me when I was with Foda. Caspar, he was lucky, he never heard them. He did not get distracted from chores like I did. He was a good boy. Although he was the second born, he was the strong one."

There was silence then. Jacob turned his face to the wall and when he spoke again, his voice was low, thick with tears.

"Dead babies, only dead babies after that for Mutta. She was slipping away from us, going to them. It made Foda so angry that she was weak, that I was weak. He needed more strong ones like Caspar to work on the farm. Mutta smiled at him and when I was nine she went to the dead babies."

Then I nearly fell off the edge of my bed because at this, Jacob sat upright and let out a wail. I was terrified that someone would hear and come running, but no one did. He just sat there, shaking. "Mutta, she did not come back. She did not talk to me, not even when I begged and begged and cried for her. Neither does Caspar. My own dead do not speak to me. For those with the gift, our own dead are silent."

Adam spoke up. "My mummy died, too. She got sick and she wouldn't let me go and get help. I made her soup, but she wouldn't eat it. She fell asleep and I thought that was good because when she woke up she would be better. Only she didn't wake up."

There were two horror stories unfolding here, both the equal of my own.

Adam looked over at Jacob, then reached a small hand toward Jacob's face and brushed away tears. "It must have been so hard," he said, "to lose your mother, but you had your father and your brother still, didn't you?"

Jacob shuddered. "Foda wanted more babies, ones who would grow strong like Caspar, so he found a new mutta, Elfrida. She was just a girl, only six years older than me. He had to travel far away to find her. The families near us would not trust Foda with their girls. The babies did not come at first, but then they did, dead ones like our mutta's. Only little Kat came, but she was a girl and that made Foda angry. Then Elfi went to join her dead babies. She talked to me after—she is not my dead. She told me that since I was twelve now, I had to look out for little Kat. We both did, Caspar and me. We kept her with us when we worked, but when she started walking, it became hard." Jacob reached out a hand, as if he was trying to pull someone toward him. "I tried to stop her, but she was too fast. She was just a little girl, three years old. She did not mean to knock over the pail of milk. He should not have hit her. She was just a little girl."

I knew it was Foda. I didn't have to ask. Even across the years, I smelled the man's anger, just like the anger Danny had. I let the pamphlet fall from my hand, felt the pleasure of my fists clenching, fought down the urge to hurt someone or something.

"Little Kat would never be safe again. Caspar and me, we knew that. We had talked. Elfi came and talked, too, but only I could hear her. We had to take Kat to Elfi's family, who lived near Dundas. I left that night. I wanted Caspar to come, too, but he said he should stay. If someone were still there to help on the farm, Foda would not want to stop working. He would not waste time looking for us.

"I walked for three days. Kat walked sometimes, but she was just a little girl, so sometimes I had to carry her. Elfi's family were sad and happy when we got to them: sad that their Elfi was dead; happy that I had brought Kat to them and that now she would be safe. They wanted me to stay, too, but I had to get back to Caspar." Jacob was panting now, like he was running a race. "I was so tired. The rain was coming so hard. I found shelter under some bushes by the side of the trail, near the water. I did not mean to sleep."

There was a silence. In the dim light, I could see that Jacob's mouth was moving, but no words were coming out. After a ragged sigh, he finally spoke. "The first blow, it woke me up." His head rocked to one side as if someone had landed a fist on his jaw. Then he flopped backward as if another punch had hit his shoulder. It was bizarre to watch Jacob's body twitch, reacting to blows that I could not see, but which he clearly felt, blows from a beating given over a hundred years ago to another boy entirely. As I watched, I saw imprints of large hands appear on Jacob's neck, red deepening to purple as the unseen hands increased the pressure.

I couldn't stop myself. I jumped forward, my hands batting uselessly at empty air. I growled with frustration, but I had done enough. Jacob's body straightened out and he coughed.

"I knew. Foda had killed Caspar. I knew his hands." He closed his eyes. "I called out to Caspar, but I heard nothing, sensed nothing. With my mind, I called and called. I had never felt so alone. I did not want to be there. So I pushed. I pushed myself as far away from my sorrow and loneliness as I could." He grimaced. "I ended up here, in this place that is loud and confusing, that does not seem real at all. I must go home to the real place. Kat needs me."

"You pushed?" I couldn't believe this. "You pushed yourself through time? You've got to be fucking kidding me! Why can't you just push yourself back?"

"I have tried! Every day I try, but I can't. Even tonight, while we waited for lights-out, I was trying."

There was no way to answer that.

Jacob turned and faced the wall again, leaving me to stare at his back and wonder what on earth I could do.

Adam had said nothing during the last part of Jacob's story, but he had been listening intently. Now he pointed at Jacob and whispered to me, "We have to help him, Mike. We just have to. Between us we can think of a way."

I admired his optimism, but I wasn't sure that we could.

I had no idea of the time, but I suspected it was early morning. Adam was already heading for the door, his forehead scrunched up as if he was thinking hard.

"You can't say anything about this, okay?" I stared hard at Adam, willing him to see that I really meant this.

"I won't. I promise. Apart from you and Mr. Mazzone, I don't really talk to anyone."

Yeah, I had to give him that. In his own way, Adam was as much of an outcast as Jacob and me.

At some point, I must have lay back down, too, because suddenly it was morning and the gong for breakfast was clanging away. I shot upright, looking around, but no Jacob. His bed was actually messed up today, sheets and blankets kicked toward the end like a real boy had slept there. He came in as I was hurriedly throwing my clothes on. He still looked weird, wispy and furtive, and kept his eyes to the ground. He moved slowly and gingerly because of the bruises, but if you looked at his face you knew that something had changed. The best way I can describe it is to say that he was like a house that had been vacant for a long time and now someone was living there.

"Shall we go downstairs now?" A small smile crept across his face.

I followed him in amazement, interested to see if he would talk to anyone but Adam and me.

Chaz was in position, presiding over the doling out of breakfast: rubbery scrambled eggs, toast, and bacon. As we sat down, he raised a questioning eyebrow but I didn't have a chance to say anything.

As he flopped down into his chair, Jacob pushed the plate bearing his usual plain roll away and without looking directly at Chaz whispered, "I would like that," pointing at the eggs.

This couldn't have had a greater effect if he'd whipped his clothes off and danced naked on the table. All conversations stopped and everyone stared at our end of the table. It was the first time most of the others had ever heard Jacob's strange, raspy voice. I swear Chaz had tears in his eyes. He didn't say anything, just ladled some of the yellow mess onto a plate and handed it to Jacob, who nodded his thanks and then settled down to eat, apparently oblivious of the stir he had caused.

Me, I was in a cold sweat. I knew that as soon as breakfast was over Chaz would be giving me the interrogation to end all interrogations. That wasn't that big a deal. What worried me more was that Jacob was going to go and announce where he'd come from to the assembled masses. If he did that, then we were in serious shit, because he'd be carted off to an asylum before you could say "real place."

Not another word passed Jacob's lips until the very end of the meal. As the emptied plates (well, there weren't actually that many of those because the eggs were truly god-awful) were passed up the table to be stacked for washing, he nodded his head again and quietly, without looking at Chaz, said, "I thank you."

Chaz was not subtle. "Err, Mike, would you give me a hand with the clearing up today?" His studiedly casual tone fooled no one.

For form's sake, I sighed and kicked my chair back hard. "Fine," I said, trying to sound bored and put-upon and anything but fine as I picked up the plates. I ignored the wet kissing sounds that Paddy was making quietly from his place at the table.

I think I half expected Jacob to follow me and Chaz into the kitchen, but, no, he slipped silently from the table, and the last view I had was of him ghosting his way up the stairs, presumably to our room.

"So?" Chaz was leaning back against the sink when I staggered in, laden with plates. "What on earth did you do? How did you get him talking?" He was grinning and it was hard not to grin back. "You do realize, don't you, that Jacob's never spoken except to answer questions before. It's amazing. We've only ever managed to get his name out of him, and that was after weeks of asking!"

Playing it down seemed to be the safest option. "He had a nightmare, started jerking around like he was being hit." It's my experience that lies work best if they have a tiny bit of the truth in them. "I just tried to get him to calm down. Nothing major, just told him that he was safe, that he didn't have to go back to school just yet." I shrugged. "I thought that, I don't know, maybe he was reliving the attack that put him in the hospital or something."

I felt like a rabbit caught in a car's headlights, so intense was Chaz's stare, the way he was willing me to somehow solve the mystery of Jacob Mueller for him. I couldn't deal with it, so I turned my back and busied myself scraping crap from the plates and loading them into the dishwasher.

"What did he say? Did he say who did it to him?"

Yeah, like I could tell Chaz what Jacob had actually said. "Nah, nothing like that. Most of the time I couldn't make out what the hell he was saying because he talks so funny, and with the crying, you know . . ."

I continued working away, and could almost feel the disappointment radiating from Chaz.

I turned around and made for the dining room to get more plates. "I did ask him." I paused in the doorway, like something had just occurred to me. "Jacob says he doesn't remember much, nothing from his life before. Only"—and here, sick bastard that I am, I paused for maximum effect—"he did say one name: Dundas." I waited, but Chaz was silent, so I carried on with the clearing up.

When I came back in with the last of the plates and dishes, Chaz hadn't moved. "Mike," he said, "are you sure he said Dundas?"

"Yeah." My mind was racing, wondering if I had said too much. I did my best to look innocent and curious. "Could that be where he's from?"

Chaz shook his head. "If it were only that simple, Mike. If that's what he said, it just adds to the mystery. It's where he was found, just outside Hamilton." The fact that Chaz was a talker and could never resist adding extra info to any conversation helped me out. "It was weird, Mike. He was found all beaten and bruised like I told you, along a hiking trail in the Dundas Valley Conservation Area, where the trail meets Sulphur Springs Road. He was right by the spout that the old spring comes out of now." Chaz laughed. "You can't miss the place because of the stink of rotten eggs."

"So, who found him?' I asked.

"A jogger out for an early morning run," Chaz said. "He was spooked, I can tell you, to see a strangely dressed kid who was beat-up and bleeding. Luckily, he had a cellphone on him and he dialed 911." He paused then, giving me a sincere look, and said, "Seriously, listen for anything you think might help. I think Jacob trusts you, okay?"

I nodded. I wanted to get out of there. There were too many questions and no answers that I could safely give. At least I had learned something: the place where Jacob had come through time.

The door to our room was shut. I thought I could hear voices, whispers coming from inside. I shuddered, feeling cold sweat form once again on my forehead. I wasn't sure that I could face hearing the voices around Jacob again. A sudden thud and the whimper that followed shook me out of my funk. I threw the door open to see Jacob huddled up on the floor, Paddy standing over him with one foot raised, preparing to kick.

I grabbed Paddy by the back of his sweatshirt and flung him aside. He lurched back toward me, fists clenched. Jacob rose shakily to his feet, his eyes never leaving Paddy. He almost hissed when he spoke, and raised one hand to point directly at Paddy. "I know what you are. You like the pain of others. It makes you forget who you are, and your own pain."

Paddy didn't like what he was hearing. His face twisted in a snarl. "Freak!" he exclaimed viciously. "You know nothing about me." When I moved menacingly toward him, he straightened up, attempted a swagger. "Remember what I said, freak. You might be talking now, but there are some things you don't talk about. Your goon," he said, flicking a dismissive finger at me, "won't always be there, and that's when I'll come for you if you talk. Remember that." His attempt at a dignified departure crumbled when he broke into a run as he passed by me on his way out of the room.

Before I could ask him if he was all right, Jacob knelt on his bed and stared out the window. "There is one in every place," he said wistfully. "One whose anger burns, makes them lash out." He sighed. "I could not stop Foda. You could not stop Danny. Maybe this one we can stop."

I didn't like the sound of this, not one fucking bit. If I had things worked out, and I thought I did, there was no need for trouble. All we needed was some time—time to plan, to gather some things, and then to try out my theory. Jacob as caped crusader against evil would screw things up royally.

Chapter Eleven

We were rousted out of our room soon after that. It's policy. Unless you're sick, you're not allowed to hole up in your room for too long—God knows what you might get up to there. Sunday dragged by, like Sundays always do in shitholes like Medlar House. Jacob had pretty much reverted to his usual silent self. Chaz mounted a one-man charm offensive in an effort to get him talking, but Jacob was having none of that. It must have been more frustrating than ever for Chaz: before, you never knew whether Jacob was actually hearing you. Now you knew he was, because he would actually answer questions, but only with his new mantra: "That I do not remember."

Paddy was never far away, watching and listening, and his smirk grew more pronounced every time Jacob professed amnesia. He obviously figured that he was safe, that Jacob wasn't going to finger him for the beating.

One interesting twist was that Matt was definitely keeping his distance from Paddy. If anything, he seemed to be trying to stay close to me. I hoped I was imagining that; another lame duck was the last thing I needed.

It was hard to fill the time. I pretended to read, but my brain was preoccupied with how to get Jacob back to what he called his "real place." I was stumped. I needed to talk to him again. My chance finally came in the late afternoon. It had been snowing on and off for most of the day. At about 4:00 p.m. it stopped, and the bitingly cold wind died down. Someone suggested going out to build a snowman and the idea was taken up en masse. Jacob obviously wanted no part of this. He had spent the afternoon sitting alone at a table in the common room; unusually, he was actually doing something today. I don't know where he got them from, but he had a pencil and some paper and had been scribbling furiously, covering the sheets protectively with his arm if anyone came within ten feet of him. Luce was going out to supervise the snow antics and stopped to ask if I was coming.

"Nah, I'll stay here, keep an eye on him," I said, nodding toward Jacob.

Luce smiled. "Careful, Mike," she said, "you'll be getting a reputation as a softie."

I didn't dignify that with a reply.

As soon as everyone was outside, I went over to Jacob. Without looking up, he said, "You have thought of a way for me to return to the real place." His voice implied absolute certainty. Great.

"I don't know," I replied. "Not yet. I don't get what you mean by 'you pushed.'"

Jacob's pencil stopped moving. He became very still. When he finally spoke, there was a tiny pause between each of his words, as if he was weighing them carefully. "Caspar was my brother, but he was also my only friend for so many years. I felt the same love for him as you do for your Jon. When I felt . . ."— there was a much longer pause here, and Jacob's voice wavered—"his life end, when I felt what Foda had done . . . part of me ended, too." He put his face in his hands for a moment. "Kat was safe, which was good, but without Caspar by my side everything in my world was black. I did not want to be there. It was like a wind, a huge wind in my head. I let it grow until it was all I could feel. Then I used that wind. I let it blow me away without caring where it would take me. I wanted so badly to be gone." Tears were forming in Jacob's eyes. He dashed them away. "Only now that I am here, I don't want to be. I want to be with Kat. I want it so badly, but I cannot make that strong wind come, only a little breeze." He looked hopefully at me.

"I think I get it," I said, "but I'm going to have to think about it some more. How to get that wind feeling back. It's not like I can beat you up, is it?" He smiled a little at that. "Anyway, if that were all it took, you would have gone back when Paddy and his thugs jumped you. Can you remember anything else, anything at all?"

"Eggs," Jacob said, "the smell of bad eggs that have been left too long in the chicken house. It came from the water. I did not drink it even though I was thirsty."

There was a commotion then in the hallway, a voice wailing about a snowball being thrown too hard, one of the littler boys crying, Luce's voice soothing.

Jacob almost seemed glad of the distraction, but he shifted his arm so that I could see the paper he had been scribbling on. Only it wasn't scribbling; it was a drawing, an amazing one, so good that it looked almost like a photograph. It showed a little girl, a toddler almost. She had long hair that had been messily braided, and wore a smock-like dress. Her feet were bare. One hand was reaching up to a larger, disembodied hand that was grasping hers tightly. It's difficult to describe the look on her face. I want to say hopeful, but there was more to it than that: concentrated, desperate, fervent. I could go on. Jacob was a brilliant artist. My spine tingled a little as I recalled the pamphlet: Kat had written that The Prophet drew likenesses of the dead.

"This is Kat," he said, "and that is my hand."

I wasn't entirely sure where he was going with this, and the hubbub in the hallway was growing as more kids trooped inside.

"Perhaps," he said, "it will help for us to see Kat, help us take my body back to her."

The whole thing was so bizarre: I didn't see that it could hurt. "Who knows, Jacob?" was all I had time to say before the others piled into the room.

I'll admit I was stymied.

Adam came over to us, cheeks pink and eyes shining. "We built a snowman." In his excitement, he sounded so much younger than he usually did. "I've never played in the snow like that before!" He dropped his voice and looked around like an actor in a bad spy movie. "Did Jacob say anything else? Do you know how we can get him back?"

"Yeah, a bit. I got him to try and explain this 'pushing' thing, and I think I get it. It's like he used his sadness, or his pain, as a wind to blow him away." Even as I said this I realized how far-fetched it sounded, but Adam was nodding like it made total sense to him.

"It's not just being sad, though, is it?" Adam was looking very serious now. "If it was that, he'd be long gone, because he must be really sad here, and when they beat him up especially." With a snort, he continued. "I wish it was that easy, because everyone who's sad or hurt could be somewhere else, right?

Only . . ." He paused, shaking his head sadly. "I don't know where else I could go."

There was something in what he said that nagged at me, but I couldn't tease it out. Not then, anyway.

The rest of Sunday was uneventful. Jacob kept to himself, drawing and being secretive about what he was doing, although no one was interested in it. I didn't bother him, just watched to make sure no one else did either. Adam was obviously still shit scared of Paddy, because he stayed close to me all day. He inveigled me into a game of chess, which at least stopped him talking all the time about his mother or, worse, asking me about mine. He got me thinking, though. I suspected that over time my mother would visit me less and less—it was too much effort for her, and I was too troublesome to her version of things —and I was okay with that. Once I aged out of the system, I wouldn't have to see her again, and I wouldn't. I didn't need her, not really. It made me think about how the three of us, Jacob, Adam and I, were all sad in our different ways for reasons having to do with our mothers. Jacob's mother loved him but died. Adam's mother loved him too much, and I had to wonder just what had caused that and what damage it had done to him, and mine, mine had not been cruel but she was careless in her love of Jon and me. Heavy stuff.

Adam beat me, not because I was distracted but

because he was really good at chess. With all the thoughts of family and mothers roiling around in my head, I also kept wondering why Adam's take on Jacob's "pushing" bothered me. There was something I was missing.

After dinner that night, when most of the others were watching TV and Jacob had gone up to our room, I sat down with Adam and set up the chessboard again, but really I just wanted to talk to him.

"Adam, you know how you said that Jacob's emotions must not be enough to let him 'push' through time. What else was there, do you think?"

As he toyed with the pawns, moving them around and then putting them back on their proper squares, Adam scrunched his face up. "My mummy read this book to me . . ."

I sighed. I really didn't want to hear any more about Mummy.

"It was about kids who time-traveled. They had to go to a special place. It was a place where there was a kind of hole."

"You mean they went into an actual hole, like a tunnel?" That wouldn't work, not from the description of the place where Jacob had been found.

"No, silly!" Adam was amused by what he obviously considered my stupidity. "They went to a place in the forest where it was like there was a hole in time itself!"

I wanted to punch the air, because it sounded like this might be it. Jacob had tried and tried to go back to his real place since arriving at Medlar House, but it never worked. Could it be that he had to be back at the same place where he first came through?

"You're from around here, aren't you?" I asked Adam, who looked puzzled at the change of subject.

"Yes, for the last two years anyway. We were somewhere else before but we had to move away quickly. Why?"

"Did your mother ever take you to the conservation area in Dundas?" It was a long shot, but Adam had mentioned that she took him to places that were free.

"Yeah. We went to the railway station they have there. It's like a museum. And we walked on some of the trails."

It was hard to keep my excitement under wraps. "Did you go anywhere where there was a sulphur spring? Where it smelled really bad?" I was holding my breath.

Adam nodded furiously. "There's a place where a road crosses one of the trails and there's a brick thing with a water pipe coming out of it. Pee-yew! It's stinky and there's yellow stuff where the water hits the bricks and the ground. Mummy said I shouldn't touch it, but when she was looking at the trail map I stuck my finger in and tasted it. It was gross!"

I stopped him there. "That's where Jacob was found. I think you've nailed it. We have to get him back there somehow! At least we can try and see if it works."

"I bet it will!" Adam's voice was rising.

I put my finger to my lips to get him to tone it down. We didn't need anyone overhearing this.

"Apart from the brick thing, I bet it's just like it was in Jacob's time. The road isn't even paved, just dirt." Adam was running with the idea and it gave me hope. "Let's tell him!"

"Not now, Adam. I'll see what he thinks tonight, okay? And no sneaking into our room. We can't do anything that might cause trouble."

He pouted a bit at that, but eventually nodded.

I went up to our room early and found Jacob sitting on the edge of his bed just staring into space. Looking up, he said, "You will get me back to Kat, yes?"

I had to respect his single-mindedness. "Maybe." I didn't want to promise something that I couldn't deliver. All I had was an idea. "Adam and I were talking about your 'pushing.' He thinks you might have to be back at the place where it first happened, by the sulphur spring."

I watched him closely as he thought about this. He smiled then, a huge, happy grin. "Yes," he said simply. "That could be." He lay down then, still smiling. "I just have to wait. Mutt will get me to the real place. Adam helped. Jon said this is how it would be."

He was smart. He'd pushed the right buttons. I thought I would have difficulty sleeping, given everything that had happened, but, no, it was like the events of the last few days had caught up with me. I was out like a light—no dreams, nothing—until morning.

Jacob had slept well, too, I could tell. His bruises were fading from thundercloud purple to yellow, and despite them, he looked better than I had ever seen him. He had lost that closed-off, haunted look, and, for the first time, he seemed to be taking in his surroundings, watching everything and everyone, touching objects like he was seeing them for the first time. When it was time for the rest of us to head off to school, he was actually sitting in front of the TV, watching something, although what he was going to make of talking aardvarks, God only knew.

Chapter Twelve

My intention for the day was to keep my head down and find out how to get to Sulphur Springs Road. The money issue was also on my mind. We were given lunch money each day to use in the cafeteria, so the obvious move was to skip lunch and pocket it, starting from that day. What can I say, I'm a big guy and it had never occurred to me to voluntarily miss a meal before. By the end of the week, I'd have twenty-five dollars and that should be enough.

Nothing else was out of the ordinary, except that Paddy, perhaps sensing my distraction, and feeling confident that Jacob wasn't going to blow the whistle on him, had a little more swagger than usual. He was more overt than he had been lately with his bullying of the others. He left me alone, but that was the only sensible thing to do. What was worrisome was that

Matt was definitely on the outs with him. Some of Paddy's shoves and gibes today were for him, and I didn't like the way Matt was hanging around me as though that would afford him some protection. When we got on the van, I had to throw my backpack down on the seat next to me when I saw Matt making like he was going to flop down there. Paddy, who was behind him, let out a psychotic giggle and elbowed him hard in the kidneys as Matt was forced into the seat behind me. Once we were at school, I stopped worrying about it. Matt and I were in completely different classes, and I didn't have to see him or think about him.

Going without lunch was hard. My stomach was screaming and twisted in knots by noon. I tried to tame it into submission by drinking water, but that didn't seem to have much effect. Distracting myself was the only thing that worked, and I used my free time to look up stuff on Mr. Halloran's computer, mapping a route from Medlar House to Sulphur Springs Road and locating the spring itself. I checked out bus routes, too, and found that we could get within about a mile of the spring, but the rest of the journey would have to be on foot. The safest way to go was through the conservation area. We would be the least likely to be spotted there, and one of the trails actually crossed the road right by the spring. I didn't risk printing anything off—Halloran was in the room, at his desk—

just made notes and drew myself a map that would be good enough.

I also started to formulate a plan—well, more of a schedule. If I didn't die of starvation, the twenty-five dollars I'd have amassed by the end of the week would cover bus fare and maybe some food should we need it. The difficulty would be getting out of Medlar House. Within reason, we were allowed out as long as we said where we were going and could accurately say when we'd be back, but somehow I didn't think anyone would let Jacob out without an adult, even if I came up with a plan to take him somewhere and offered to be his guide and guardian. So that ruled out the weekend; there would be a hell of a ruckus if I tried to spirit Jacob away then. I was going to have to sneak him out after lights-out some night and then hope I could get back before anyone noticed that we'd gone. I thought Friday night would be best, since we were allowed to sleep in until nine if we wanted to on Saturdays. Adam, of course, couldn't come; his room-mate would raise the alarm. I wasn't looking forward to telling him that, nor was I sure how patient Jacob was going to be, but at least I would be giving him a timeline.

If we did manage to get out and the plan, unlikely as it seemed, worked all around, I decided that if I got back unseen, I was going to swear that Jacob had taken off under his own steam in the night without waking me up. No one would be able to prove otherwise, and I would just have to withstand a couple of days of questions from everyone before it was all just added to the mystery of Jacob Mueller.

I'm sure you've heard the phrase "the best laid plans of mice and men." Yeah, nothing worked out, and that's why I am stuck here trying to sort it all out in my head, trying to decide what I can say when I finally start talking to the cops.

It would be easy to blame it all on Paddy. I've kind of been setting him up as the villain through all this, but you know what, it wasn't just him. Jacob started things, and, God help me, I finished them. That's probably what's going to do me in.

Everything seemed routine after school. Jacob was in the van with Chaz when he came to pick us up, and you could tell that Chaz was thrilled about this. For all I know, old Jacob had been talking up a storm all day, though I somehow doubted it. He stuck close to me when we got back to Medlar House, not saying much. Adam was waiting in the hallway when we walked in. I felt like the leader of a pack of small, annoying dogs.

While the others watched television, we sat down at the table and got the chess set out. Adam and I made a half-hearted effort at playing while Jacob watched. What I really wanted to do was tell them about the plan I had come up with and what my research at school had turned up.

To say they liked my scheme was the understatement of the year. Adam in particular was all over it.

"I never spend my allowance, Mike. You can have it. I have fifteen dollars. I'll go get it now. We can . . ."

I put my hand up, trying to get him to pipe down before he got so excited that people started noticing. "Adam, I'm sorry, but you can't come." Thank God he didn't protest loudly or, worse, start to cry. He just looked at me miserably. I felt so mean. I tried to explain: "You have a roommate. He'll report you missing."

"No, no," Adam insisted, keeping his voice low. "I'll beg him not to."

"We can't take the risk. I promise I'll be back before it's time to get up in the morning. I won't let you down." This sounded feeble even to me.

Jacob spoke then, which surprised us both. Our surprise grew when he leaned toward Adam and took his hand where it was resting next to the chessboard. "Adam, your mother has told me where you must go. You have a grandfather, her father, who helped her hide you by sending money to her. She meant to tell you, tell you his name and where he lives, but she had no time. She got so sick, so very sick, so fast."

Adam's mouth hung open. "She never said. She told me we were all alone."

I couldn't tell whether the look on his face was anger or sadness.

"Once a month, she got a letter," Adam continued. "A small brown envelope. I asked her about it, but she said it was just a magazine. She was lying to me."

It was definitely anger now.

"She says she did not mean to hurt you, Adam." Jacob was awkwardly patting the smaller boy's hand. "She believed that there were people who would do harm to both of you. It was not a true belief, though, not at all. It came from a sick place in her mind. But Mike will help you. He will help you pretend that you have just remembered about your grandfather now. You have been sad and it has been hard, and they will believe that you have only just remembered."

Mike the hero, rescuer of young orphans and lost time-travelers! I suppose I should have been flattered that they both had so much faith in me.

It did the trick: Adam accepted that he would not be coming with us, that I would come back and help get him out of Medlar House, too. He scooted off to his room to fetch his stash of money.

At dinner, Jacob was not only calm, he was positively voluble, asking for more mashed potatoes and even giving Chaz something other than "That I do not remember" when he asked if potatoes had always been one of his favorites. With a sly glance at me, he said, "Yes, I have always liked them. I have liked them for a very long time."

When it was time for bed, everyone headed upstairs.

Lights-out came and went, and I was drifting off to sleep when Jacob got up and said he had to go to the bathroom.

I was dozing, so I didn't think about it at first, but after a while I realized that he'd been gone about ten minutes. I listened, but it seemed quiet in the hall. I was just about to go look for him when our bedroom door opened and Matt's white face appeared.

"Mike," he whispered, "come quickly. Jacob's gone mad. He's going after Paddy."

"What?" This made no sense at all.

"Come on!" Matt was already heading back out the door. "They're in the bathroom."

I didn't wait to hear more, just followed Matt. By "they," I thought he had meant Paddy and Jacob, but Adam was there, too, huddled in a corner, clutching his bleeding nose.

Thank God they weren't making a lot of noise. We didn't need Chaz or Bob coming up to find out what was going on. Judging from the sounds coming from downstairs, they were deep into some loud film.

God knows what had possessed Jacob. Even afterward I couldn't get much out of him, just that here we could stop Paddy, when we had both failed before. I knew he was referring to his foda and to Danny, but to me it seemed like a major overreaction to put Paddy in the same category as those two. He was a bully, that's all. I don't know. Maybe that psychic stuff was at work, and Jacob saw the potential for big-time violence in him. You know what, it doesn't matter. It happened. There's no going back.

I think Jacob had gone into the bathroom and found Paddy tormenting Adam. Surprise might have been on his side at the beginning, but by the time Matt and I got there, he was getting hammered. Paddy had pinned him to the floor, a knee on either side of his torso, and was slapping his face, rocking his head from side to side, punctuating each slap with a hissed "Fucking freak!" Jacob was fighting back, bucking and twisting, trying to get free, but Paddy outweighed him and he had no chance.

To be honest, I don't have a clear grasp of what happened next. I am not trying to weasel out of it. I beat Paddy up. I know that, and I know that it was bad, that it went on longer than it should have, and that I was trying to hurt him. But it's like I was watching it happen, and even if I had wanted to stop, I couldn't. At one point, he was on his feet and I was punching him with all my strength, almost enjoying the meaty thwack of my fists on his flesh. Then he was on the floor, and I was kicking him. He was out of it by then, wasn't even trying to defend himself, just a limp meat puppet, jerking with each blow.

It took all three of them to stop me. Jacob, still on the floor, grabbed my legs, clasping them firmly so I had to stay rooted to the spot or risk hurting him, too. Matt and Adam dragged Paddy to one side. As my breathing slowed down, I started to feel sick, especially when I looked at Paddy. His face was covered with blood. By the whistling sound of his breathing, I knew I'd broken his nose. He was out cold.

"Shit," Matt said in a shaken voice. "I just wanted you to stop him." He shuddered. "You're as bad as he is. What the fuck are we going to do? He needs a doctor. You're going to be gone after this."

The staccato sentences were doing my head in. "Shut up, Matt," I snapped. I needed time to think. "Look, it's bad, I know, but I'm going to get Jacob out of here."

Matt's face was closed and cold. I invoked the magic word then. I had to, and what I said was even true in a way. "I know how to get him back to his family. Give us two hours, just enough time to get away." I was pleading, and I knew that I sounded desperate, that there was no logic to what I was asking for, no reason why he should help us. "I can't tell you or anyone else how I am going to do this. No one would believe me. Please, Matt, let at least one of us get back to where we should be, to family."

I could tell he was thinking, taking me seriously.

"Once I've done that, I'll come back, take my lumps. Please."

I still don't know whether he would have agreed based on what I had said, but Jacob spoke then, and that swung it. "Trust him, Matt. He is not bad, not deep down. He is going to help me, look after me, like your grandmother tried to look after you. She told me that when your mother could not care for you, she did, even though people said she was too old. Mike will help Adam find his family, too."

Hearing this, Matt looked even shakier. "Go," he said, his voice a choked whisper. "Help me get him back to our room. I'll call for help in two hours, no more. Make sure you're long gone by then."

It took all four of us to lift Paddy; he was a dead weight. He stirred and groaned, but didn't come to as we carried him back to the bedroom he shared with Matt.

"C'mon, Jacob, we've got to move fast." I was ushering him out the door when Adam called me back. "Wait! We have to make it look like Matt had no part in this. Tie him to that chair."

I felt like this was wasting time, but I could see his point. I ripped the sheets off the bed and tied Matt's legs and arms to the chair.

I flicked the light switch off as we left the room and tried to shut out that croaky breathing. How could I have done that? How much like Danny was I?

Chapter Thirteen

It was surprisingly easy to get out of Medlar House. I got Jacob bundled up into as many clothes as I could. He didn't argue. He must have known that all our planning had gone out the window after what I'd done to Paddy and that we had to move now if he had a chance of getting to his real place.

We were probably helped by the fact that Chaz and Bob were really into what sounded like some space crap on the TV, something with lots of fighting and techno noises. We slid past the TV room and I opened the closet near the door to get our coats. Between Adam's allowance and my lunch money, I hoped I had enough for our bus fare and something to eat, but I wasn't sure. I recognized Chaz's beat-up leather jacket in the closet, and I knew he kept his wallet in the inside pocket. It was so tempting to lift it and take whatever money was there, but I just couldn't do it. Chaz had been nothing but good to us. I was already going to disappoint him with what I'd done to Paddy. I couldn't add to it. I prayed that I would get a chance to explain things—well, some sort of version of them—to him when it was all over.

It was cold outside, bone-chillingly cold. I had no idea of the time, but it must have been about 11:00 p.m. We had to get as far away from Medlar House as we could in the two hours that Matt had promised us. I hoped and prayed that he might give us longer, might even wait out the night, but I doubted that would happen. He was scared about the damage I'd done to Paddy, and he would start yelling for help sooner rather than later. To be honest, I was scared, too, not just about Paddy's condition, but that I did what I did to him in the first place. I'm a self-described thug, but until then I'd always had boundaries that I wouldn't cross. Now everything had changed. The only certainty I had left was that I had to get Jacob out of there. Jon had told him I could save him and I had to do it. I just had to pray that I could get it done before the hunt for us really got under way. Shit, there was Adam to think of, too. Why hadn't Jacob told him his grandfather's name? Had he concealed it earlier to make sure that I kept my promise and didn't back out of our plan?

"Mike, how do we get to the stream?" Jacob was gamely trotting at my side, even though his bruised body must have been protesting at the punishing pace I was setting.

"Bus to Dundas, okay? Then we walk." I was scanning the street, hoping that not too many people would be out at this time of night. My size meant that I would be taken for an adult unless you got close, but since Jacob looked so much younger than he was, people would wonder what he was doing out so late. Mind you, I didn't want anyone getting too close to me for any reason: my face—once seen, never forgotten. Then I remembered I had my hat in my coat pocket, only it wasn't really a hat, more like a ski mask and a hat in one. Lucy had given it to me. She hadn't made a big deal out of it, didn't say why she'd chosen this particular style, but it was obvious and now I thanked her for it. With it on, and in the right light, you really couldn't see the scar. Hollow cheek, pulled-up mouth: it was all pretty much hidden. Yeah, if you were observant, you might notice more, but most people aren't, and with my collar pulled up, I was just a guy trying to keep warm on a bitter night.

Beyond the bus, I had no plan. I'd been expecting to have four days to think this through, not to have to go on the run. Another ten minutes of walking would take us to McNab Street, where there was a kind of bus terminal. It would be a straightforward ride to the stop at the outskirts of Dundas; from there, we could walk to the conservation area. Or so I thought.

My aim was to have as little conversation with other people as possible. I didn't want to make it easy to track our movements later via anyone we had any interaction with. So once we found the bus stop, I scanned the schedules till I found the bus I thought would take us to the right place. An empty bus was sitting there waiting, engine running. I pulled Jacob on, paid for our tickets and then sat us down near the middle. At least it was warm.

I was hoping that the bus would get some other passengers—otherwise we were going to be so noticeable—and as we wound through downtown Hamilton it did: a couple of guys who'd obviously been drinking; some girls, students maybe, or nurses from the hospital, the one where Jacob had been taken. The drunk guys were a godsend. They were raucous, trying to chat up the girls, giving them cheesy lines. It was all good-humored and the girls were laughing, and it was just the protective noise that Jacob and I needed.

I'd calculated that our stop would be the fourth one we got to after the bus reached Dundas, but just after we entered the town, the bus stopped and the driver shouted out, "End of the line."

What? This was bogus. I didn't want to ask him

what was going on, so I got up and, Jacob trailing behind me, got off. The bus had pulled onto a side street, near what looked like an apartment block. I could see the lights of a small plaza a little way off, a donut shop still lit up.

"Excuse me," I said to one of the guys who'd been on the bus with us, staying as far back in the shadows as I could, "doesn't this bus go out to Davidson Boulevard? My brother and I are going to stay there at our aunt's tonight."

He laughed. "Better start walking, boys. That's only until about 7:00 p.m. If you've got a cellphone, I'd call your aunt to come and get you. It's quite a ways and all uphill. If you don't, there's a phone over in the plaza."

"Thanks," I said.

"Mike?" Jacob was huddling close to me. He was shivering and his face was white and pinched with cold, making his bruises all the more prominent. Between the two of us, I wasn't sure who would draw more attention from strangers.

"Look, Jacob. The bus doesn't go as far as I thought. We're going to have to walk to the stream, but it's a long walk, so maybe we should get some food over there first." I gestured toward the donut shop with my head. "We don't want people to look at us. We don't want anyone to try and stop us. I want you to listen carefully and do exactly what I say, okay?"

He nodded. The trust I could see on his face and his hopeful expression were sort of heartbreaking.

"When we go in, I want you to find the table that is farthest away from any other people and I want you to sit with your back to the window. Keep your head down, like you're tired. Maybe even rest your head on your arms. Can you do that?"

He nodded again.

"If anyone speaks to you, don't answer. Let me do the talking." I didn't want anyone hearing his strange voice and accent. "I'll get the food and bring it over."

Jacob was as good as his word. A couple of the tables near the counter were occupied, but there was a whole bank of empty ones along the aisle that led to the bathrooms, and that's where he went. At the counter, I ordered two large hot chocolates and four donuts. I wanted to take some food with us, but I thought it would be suspicious if I ordered more—four donuts was about standard for two teenage boys, I thought. I could manage those alone on a good day. As I stood under the shop's bright fluorescent lights, the woman at the counter stared at me. She wasn't trying to hide it, either. "What happened to your face?" she asked.

"Car accident," I mumbled and looked down like I was embarrassed.

She had the hide of a rhinoceros, didn't take the hint at all. "Must have been a pretty bad one, eh?"

Still looking down, I grunted. Maybe that was my mistake, because she started up with more questions. "Isn't it kind of late for you and your kid brother to be out by yourselves?"

Shit.

I stuck to the story I'd started with the guy from the bus, only now I had to embroider it a little, maybe make her feel sorry for us, enough that she'd leave us alone. "We live in Hamilton. Our mom is sick, so we're going to stay with our aunt. She lives out on Davidson. We took the bus from the hospital, only we didn't know it wouldn't go all the way down there at night."

Her face was softening.

I kept going. I wanted to get us out of there as soon as possible. "We called her and she's coming to get us." I noticed a supermarket opposite the donut shop. "She's meeting us in the parking lot at the grocery store over there."

I grabbed the bag of donuts and the drinks and called out to Jacob. "Come on, Jon, we've got to go and meet Auntie Kat," I said, hoping and praying that he would be quick enough on the uptake to just move.

He was. Thrusting a hot chocolate into his hands, I hustled him out of the shop as quickly as I could.

"We're going to walk, okay? The sooner we can get off the streets and into the conservation area the better."

Jacob said nothing, just doggedly followed me as I started up the hill, his hands wrapped around the warmth of the cup of hot chocolate.

Later, I got to see more of Dundas, but then it was just a long road lined with apartment blocks at first, then houses. When we started walking, the buildings were close together, but after a while, the spaces between them grew larger and larger. When I finally saw the sign for the conservation area, it seemed like we'd been walking for hours.

It was spooky. There was a light layer of snow on the ground, but clumps of dry brown grass poked through. We climbed yet another hill. From the map I had seen online, I knew we'd come to an old railway station and from there we had to follow something called the Rail Trail, and it would take us to Sulphur Springs Road.

There was a light on in the station, but I was pretty sure it was only for security and that no one would be inside.

"I walked here," Jacob said, his voice floating on the cold air, "but there was no building in the real time, just trees."

I gave him a sidelong glance.

"My feet remember," he said, "even if my eyes do not."

"Come on, let your feet keep remembering," I said, a little more roughly than I intended. He freaked me out when he got mystical like that.

It was very still. All we heard was the odd rustle in the trees as an animal moved. Once, a coyote howled, but it was a long way away and sounded as if it was on the escarpment above us. Jacob was moving faster now. Sometimes he shot out ahead of me, almost as if he knew where we were going.

The road, when we came to it, wasn't much to look at. It was unpaved and ridged where water had carved runnels into the dirt. Ice had formed in the crevices, making it hard going. Before I could tell Jacob that we had to make a left turn, he had already pivoted in that direction. He was almost running now, and I had to jog to keep up with him.

"I can feel it," he gasped. "The real place is near. We must hurry. Kat needs me."

As we approached what was left of the spring, the acrid smell of bad eggs was everywhere. It was just as Adam had described it. We saw a low brick oblong; a thin metal tube jutted out from one end. The stinking water was trickling from there, staining the ground a creamy yellow where it fell.

Jacob fell to his knees in front of it, heedless of the snow. "Here," was all he said. "I lay down here."

He reached into his coat and pulled out his drawing of Kat. Then he lay down on his side, making a pillow for his cheek with his hands, still holding the drawing, looking for all the world like he was lying on the most comfortable of beds.

I didn't know what I was supposed to do, whether I needed to do anything.

"Mutt," Jacob said quietly. His eyes were open and he was looking up at me. "This will work, won't it?"

It was the first time Jacob had been anything but certain about this. My heart felt like it was breaking. I couldn't speak. After all that had happened, we couldn't fail.

Jacob smiled. "Jon said you would help me, and you have. It will work, but I am leaving you too many troubles. Adam, he needs you, too. He is lost and you must help him be found."

I fell to my knees beside him. I shook my head. "It doesn't matter," I said. The words hurt my throat and I didn't want to say them. "You have to go back to Kat, and grow up to be a man in your real place so that I can read about you in mine." I couldn't bring myself to tell him that I doubted I would be allowed back at Medlar House after what I had done.

"You have a good heart, Mike. Jon knew it and loved you for it. Your life will not be easy, but never forget me, never forget that you saved me." He closed his eyes, then reached up with one hand and closed mine, his touch gentle, a benediction. I could hear his light breathing, my name whispered, and then silence.

When I opened my eyes, the darkness was fading and the first flickers of dawn were gleaming on the bare branches of the trees.

Jacob was gone.

His drawing of Kat lay next to me. I saw that he had written something on it in large, spidery letters: Adam's name, and then another name, Jimmy Bentley. It looked as if it had been written in a hurry. There was a partial address, too, 41 Grange Road. I hoped it would be enough and that I would be able to get the information to Adam. When I picked the drawing up to put it in my pocket, I realized there was another drawing underneath.

It was Jon, and he was smiling at me.

So, there it is.

Now I have to decide what to do.

I have to pay for what I did to Paddy. There's no escaping that.

I've had a lot of time to think about what I did. The losing control, the damage I did, they scare the shit out of me. I have to believe that it was a one-off. I am not like Foda. I am not like Paddy. I am not Danny. Jacob said that I wasn't. I have to believe that. After all, he was right about everything else.

I can't tell them the truth: that I took a boy who had slipped through time back to the place where it happened in the hope that it would happen again, and that it did, but I don't know how. If I do, I'll be in the loony bin before you can say Jacob Mueller.

I will tell them that we set out together, that Jacob wanted to run away because he wasn't safe, that I beat Paddy up after he attacked Jacob. I'm praying that Matt will back me up on this. I think he will. Then my story admittedly becomes a little far-fetched. I will tell them that we were heading toward Kitchener, that Jacob had finally come clean and told me that he had relatives there, but that we got on the wrong bus.

That we were tired and camped out and that when I woke up, Jacob was gone.

It will be some time before the questions stop, but they will never find anything to disprove my story. The mystery that was Jacob Mueller will fade from everyone's mind. I don't doubt that it will get raked up from time to time, that my name will come up, that insinuations will be made about what happened. I can deal with that.

Do I have regrets? Some, for sure. First of all, Paddy. What I did will always haunt me. I have to make sure that I never lose control like that again. Then there's Chaz. He's one of the good guys in all this. I am sorry that I can't explain it all to him. He deserves to know who Jacob was and what really happened to him. I hate that Chaz probably thinks badly of me now. Adam is another worry. I have the means to help him get to safety and out of a system that will only damage him further, but I am unsure that I'll be able to tell him what he needs to know to make that happen.

It's going to be tough, but I can handle it. I have to. I can handle it because I know that this time I didn't fail. This time, I saved someone.